BITTER REVENGE

It was sheer bad luck that, when Carla's life had just about reached rock bottom, she should find herself at the mercy of the forbidding Blaze Douglas, who held her responsible for his young brother's death. Was this, though, her chance to prove to him how wrong he was about her?

BITTER REVENGE

BY

LILIAN PEAKE

MILLS & BOON LIMITED
15–16 BROOK'S MEWS
LONDON W1A 1DR

First published 1982
Australian copyright 1982
Philippine copyright 1982
This edition 1982

© Lilian Peake 1982

ISBN 0 263 73784 5

Set in Monophoto Baskerville 11 on 11½ pt.

Made and printed in Great Britain by
Richard Clay (The Chaucer Press) Ltd,
Bungay, Suffolk

CHAPTER ONE

THE towpath felt hard beneath Carla's feet. She was taking her evening walk and she rarely altered her route. There was a house which drew her, time and again. It was across the river on the other side of the weir. The rushing water divided her from it, from the occupants of the house, so effectively that the weir might just as well have been the Niagara Falls.

As Carla walked, she felt the rhythms all around her—the river's strong flow, the moorhens' business-like pace, the chicks following their mother in perfect harmony. The bushes stirred, the trees towered, the birds darted from take-off to land, only to fly again. Her own rhythms were slower. There was no one, nothing to hurry for.

Small boats clustered against the river bank. Tree branches spread across the path and Carla pushed them aside as she walked.

Not much farther now, she encouraged herself. It was a long walk, really, but she never minded that. There was little else for her to do. Her home consisted of a small cabin cruiser—battered, rusting, but a haven in the situation in which circumstances had placed her.

The boat belonged to her friend Patricia's brother. He had lost his interest in river cruising the moment he had found himself a girl-friend whose father had bought her a yacht. So his small boat, called *River Lady*, had stayed neglected at its mooring—until his sister told him of Carla's plight.

Homeless as she was, Carla did not care that little maintenance had been carried out on the vessel for a long time. What were streaks of rust, a blocked wastepipe, a berth that was hard to sit on and even harder to sleep on?

Carla's footsteps slowed and stopped. There across the water was the shining white riverside mansion, with its pillars and chimneys and windows looking over a river view that must have gratified the senses of any person living there.

As Carla stared, river craft passed, keeping to a lane which took them well away from the pull of the weir. She heard its rushing sound, its white flurry of foam, saw the low footbridge over the dancing waters from which fishermen often dangled their lines, leaning on the rail, infinitely patient.

The house riveted her gaze. She found herself resenting slightly its remote and brooding air which seemed to hide secrets. It held to itself the most precious secret of all—whether or not its owner was in residence.

She knew the owner's identity, but all she remembered about him was a pair of winter-grey eyes blazing down at her in a fury which made her flinch even now, although three years had passed since that terrible night. Moving to allow an entwined couple to go by, she pushed back her long red-gold hair.

Her time for looking was almost over. She must make the most of the few moments left. If she stayed any longer, people would think it strange . . . There was a time-switch in her mind. She had been seventeen and Crispin Douglas twenty-two.

He had asked her to marry him and she had

accepted, with a complete and youthful certainty that their married life together could bring nothing but happiness. Her parents, she had discovered, had other ideas. It would never work, they had told her. His parents were wealthy. Being the younger of the two sons, he had been over-indulged, given everything he wanted. What was more, they'd added, her nature was entirely out of tune with his.

Carla had ignored her parents' advice and continued to go out with Crispin. She had worn his ring even at home, closing her eyes to her parents' anxious glances at each other. With his own parents' money he had bought car after car, each one more powerful and more expensive than the last. His parents had given and given again, and he never questioned his right to take from them.

He had rarely spoken of his older brother. When he did, it was to abuse him. 'He went as high as he could academically,' Crispin had said with a vehemence which astonished Carla, 'then, to show everyone just how brilliant he was, he actually put all the academic rubbish he'd learnt to practical use!'

'You mean he started work in industry?' she had asked.

'"Started work"? That wouldn't have been good enough for my brother Blaze. He had to start at the top, and the only way he could do that was to form his own company and become its chief executive.'

'Straight from university?'

'That's what I said,' Crispin had replied in his jealous little-brother voice. 'Oh, let's stop talking about Blaze. He's abroad, anyway. Come on, kiss me—no, not like that, like this.' He had proceeded to kiss her in a way that had sickened her.

It was then that the seed of doubt which her parents' rationalising had implanted in her had taken root. As Crispin's lovemaking had grown more demanding—and, she was beginning to learn even with her limited experience, more selfish—those doubts plagued her.

Their unequal relationship was beginning to affect Crispin's everyday behaviour. The more she failed to respond to Crispin's sulky, 'Let yourself go. You *are* my fiancée,' the more reckless his driving had become. When she had told him he frightened her with the chances he took amongst the traffic pile-ups, the more he laughed at her fears and the faster he went.

The night Carla decided to tell Crispin she wanted to break their engagement, Crispin gave a party at his parents' house. They were away for the weekend, he'd said. The domestic staff would provide the food and clear away afterwards.

Carla had been impressed by his careless reference to 'domestic staff'. To her, having been reared by parents who lived simply, and who, even if they had wanted to, could not have afforded to have done otherwise, such words as Crispin used spelt the stuff of which films, books and dreams were made.

He had taken her only occasionally to the family residence, a few miles from the town in which she lived with her parents. The River Thames flowed by at the end of the garden. The lawn sloped to a mooring place, meeting the river.

The luxury which greeted her brown eyes stole her breath, but it did nothing to alter her resolve. She would tell Crispin of her decision not to marry him, but first she would enjoy the party to the full.

The house itself was worth staying for. Its exterior was as impressive as the out-of-this-world interior. The white walls were dazzling and balconied windows overlooked the river, white columns supporting the roof of a covered walk the length of the house. It was the house of her dreams, and in the three years since she had attended that party within its graceful white walls it had appeared and reappeared in her recurring dreams which, because of the events which followed the party, turned always and unfailingly, into a nightmare.

It was almost dark when Carla stepped down into the boat. The breeze had strengthened and the river was choppy, making the small vessel rock alongside the river bank.

The mooring rope was knotted round a tree. It was not an official mooring place, but Carla hoped that her luck, which had held for the four weeks she had been there, would not run out and that she would not be discovered. To hire an official mooring cost money, and that was a commodity of which she was short.

It had all happened at once. On the same day as she had lost her job, she had also lost her place to live.

'I've decided to retire early, Miss Howard,' her employer had told her. 'This afternoon I'm closing this shop and it will stay closed. I'm sorry, my dear,' he had added, seeing her shock.

'It's—it's very unexpected, Mr Hulton,' Carla had answered, her mind momentarily confused.

'Well,' he leaned forward on the counter and fiddled with an electrical component with which his shop was stocked, 'for some years my wife has wanted us to visit our son and his family in Australia. I only wish I had the money to keep this place on, so that you could keep your job.'

Her job! It was only then that the truth of the situation hit her. When the shop was closed that evening for the last time, her job would go with it.

'I'll give you two weeks' pay in lieu of notice, Miss Howard. I hope that will see you through until you find other employment.'

Stunned, Carla had gone home to the house she had shared with her brother and his girl-friend. Her brother had been there alone. He listened as she told him about the loss of her job, but apart from a lift of his shoulders and the brief, unsympathetic dismissal contained in the words, 'That's life,' she had received no sympathy from him.

Instead, he had gone on to say. 'I've got news for you, too. Pauline's pregnant——'

'Why, that's great!' Carla had responded.

'Thanks,' Nigel had replied. 'So we're getting married. Which means we want this place to ourselves.'

'You don't mean you want me to go?'

'Sorry. It's only a small house, and Pauline wants to make your room into a nursery.'

'Where am I suppose to live?' she had demanded in dismay. 'I've just lost my job, so where will I get the money from to pay the more realistic rent I'll be charged by someone else? Not to mention paying for food and clothing.'

'Take everything that's due to you financially as an unemployed, homeless person.' Carla had reached the door when her brother said, 'We'll give you a week or two to look round for a place.'

'Thank you kindly,' Carla had retorted, 'but have *you* tried lately getting decent living accommodation? At a price low enough for someone without an income?'

Carla had visited her friend Patricia, whose brother had been in the room when she had told her story, and at once he had offered her the use of his boat. Without hesitation, she had accepted, regardless of the fact that she knew nothing about boats, except that they floated.

'I'll be honest,' Derrick had said, 'it needs attention. I bought it third hand, but at least it will be a roof over your head.'

A roof over her head! Carla looked up now at the rust-spots, at the torn berth cushions, the general air of neglect—and closed her eyes. To her it was home, although how long it would remain so without the vital maintenance it required was questionable.

Her only illumination was an oil lamp, but its light was sufficient to allow her to read and when it was time, to wash in the small bowl and prepare for bed. Instinct told her to remove few of her clothes. In fact, the nights were sometimes so cold she piled on sweaters in addition to the blankets.

Lying on the bunk, Carla heard the night-time noises. There were rustles from the bank, scuffles amongst the bushes, the slap of the river water against the boat's sides, growing louder as she tried to sleep.

But sleep would not come because, yet again, the past had returned to haunt her.

The party had been rowdy, the food the house-keeper had provided was eaten and more had taken its place. There was a wine bar and no sooner were bottles emptied than others took their place. Couples vanished from the main party room and, after a time, returned. Others disappeared in the same way. Crispin had pulled Carla closer as they danced.

'You haven't seen my bedroom, darling, not here in my parents' house. Come on, I'll show it to you.'

Carla had known what he had meant, and it wasn't a conducted tour of the Douglas residence. She had pulled away from his arms. 'I'm not in that kind of mood,' she had protested.

'You never are,' Crispin had complained. 'Look, you are my fiancée. I'm entitled to something in payment for that ring I've given you.'

'I'm not going to marry you, Crispin,' she had answered quietly.

At first he hadn't believed her. Then he had blustered, saying he could force her upstairs if he wanted. There were plenty of his friends around who'd help him. When she had managed at last to persuade him she had meant what she said, he had sulked all the way to the wine table.

While he had drummed his fingers, impatient to be served, Carla had handed him the ring. He had been furious at her action, taking it and pushing it back into place.

'Do me a favour and pretend we're still engaged until the party's over,' he'd said. 'I've got my pride.'

So she had let the ring stay, saying, 'I'll give it back to you tomorrow, then.'

'I'm going to get drunk,' Crispin had declared, his mood sulky, 'and you're getting drunk with me.' The least she could do, Carla decided, was humour him. Maybe it was the first time in his life he'd been denied anything.

Without protest, she accepted the drink he gave her. It was stronger than the kind she was used to. When she tried to drink it slowly, having one glass to his two or three, he had grumbled, pouring more into her glass to join what was left. So she had sipped her way through that. Others came to talk, and she did her best to look absorbed in what they were saying.

Her glass was on the way to the table when she noticed it had been filled yet again. 'Crispin, I'd like to go home now. If you don't feel like taking me, I'm sure someone else——' When she saw his pout of battered pride, she knew it was the worst thing she could have said.

'It's my party,' he had grumbled childishly, 'I brought you, I'll take you home. What do you think I am, drunk and incapable?'

If only, at that moment, she had answered, 'Yes, that's what I do think', the misery and tragedy that would have been saved!

'One more dance before we go,' he demanded petulantly, and she did not resist, although she doubted his ability to move more than a few paces without lurching.

Fortunately, the tempo was slow, Crispin leant heavily against her. She was still sad about the hurt to his pride. It was nothing more, she knew for certain. Readily she gave him her support, heavy though he was.

Then Carla experienced a strange feeling of being watched. Somewhere, there was an unfriendly presence, but although she looked about her, she could not find the source. As each couple neared the door, they glanced outside and became silent, then having passed, they joked and danced and kissed uninhibitedly. Whoever or whatever that 'presence' was, she decided, it appeared to have no intention of joining the fun.

Crispin's head drooped to Carla's shoulder and her cheek rested with a rush of sympathy on his hair. She felt, if anything, like a protective sister. As the dance ended, he straightened, then tripped over her feet. He cursed and her arm went round his waist.

'Now will you take me home, Crispin?' she pleaded.

His shrug was exaggerated and jerky. 'If you must spoil the fun . . .' He took her arm and propelled her into the entrance hall. 'Won't be long, everybody,' he shouted. 'Just taking my fiancée home.' There were shouts of acknowledgement.

Crispin opened his car door. It was, as usual, a sports model, longer and lower than ever. He came round to Carla's side, lurching in a way that alarmed her.

'Where the hell are you going, Crispin?' The voice was crisp, authoritative and angry.

'Taking my fiancée home,' Crispin answered sulkily.

'No, you're not,' the man in the doorway declared.

'Is that your brother?' Carla had whispered to Crispin who had nodded.

'Some brother,' Crispin had answered, speaking with difficulty.

'He doesn't look much like you,' Carla had remarked, knowing now who the presence had been that had taken the laughter from the other guests' eyes.

'No, he's a great handsome brute—emphasis on

"brute", or so the women tell me.' Crispin looked down at himself. 'I stopped short where he went on growing. And I like my food. And drink,' he added unnecessarily. Unlocking the passenger door, he shouted, 'You can't stop me, Blaze. It's my car.'

Blaze Douglas had started to walk towards them. Carla so dreaded being in the elder brother's company even for the relatively short drive home that she darted round to the other side and flung herself into the driving seat. Blaze stopped, but even in the light which streamed from the windows of the large, white house, she could see the suppressed anger in the lean angles of his body.

Crispin shouted at Carla, 'Get out of there! *I'm* driving!'

'Just a little way, darling,' she pleaded, hoping the endearment would help to salve his pride. 'I've never driven such a wonderful car as this. Please . . .'

'Oh, well, just a short distance.' He eased himself into the passenger seat as if it was degrading for him, the owner, to take second place.

Carla dipped her head to glance through the driver's window. Her eyes were lit with a swift, bold triumph as they met the stony glance of Crispin's forbidding brother.

Crispin watched as she fastened her seat-belt. He omitted to do likewise. 'Now mind how you go,' Crispin instructed, his speech slurred.

That piece of advice, thought Carla, was rich, considering the impairment of his own judgment by an excess of alcohol. When the ignition fired with a roar, he shouted that her foot was too hard on the accelerator. Easing off, she listened as he gave the briefest of instructions on driving the powerful car.

As it moved forward, she felt she had under her control the damage potential of a giant-sized truck. Gripping the steering wheel—which was, she knew, the worst thing she could do—she tried but failed to persuade herself that she was both mentally and physically capable of driving such a vehicle. Also, there was no doubt about it, the amount of drink she herself had been coerced into taking was having an effect on her reaction time. Yet if she handed over to Crispin . . .

In the end she had no choice. He told her he would take over and willingly, she let him. Her hands shook as she fastened the seat-belt. She had urged Crispin to fasten his, but he had refused. Impatience with her own driving performance had added itself to his usual risk-taking habits, and these had, in turn, been augmented by too much drink.

The part Carla dreaded most was the long, steep descent to the outskirts of the Buckinghamshire town in which she lived. As they approached the summit and the hill swept down and away under the street lighting, Crispin cried, 'Hold on to your seats, folks, here we go!'

Terrified, Carla did just that. She glanced at her companion. He was hunched over the wheel and she could almost see the 'little boy' part of his mind taking over. Their speed increased, passing the legal limit, and Carla mauled her lower lip in an effort to suppress her cry of fear.

It was she who saw the stationary car. There was a man in overalls, looking in the boot, which indicated that the car had broken down, otherwise it wouldn't have been there.

Crispin, lost in his childlike world of toy cars hitting walls and bouncing off, had not seen it. Their speed was so fast that Carla's scream to 'mind that car' came only seconds before it registered in Crispin's mind that danger loomed.

Too late to signal overtaking, too late to do anything, since Crispin was petrified into immobility. Desperate to avoid the terrible inevitability of the fate which was awaiting them, Carla reached across, grabbed the steering wheel and wrenched it. The car had mounted the grass verge. At a crazy angle, it bumped and jumped and rolled over and over, flinging around its occupants as if they were dice in a rattling holder. Down the hill it went, bouncing and rolling until the raised bank of which the grass-covered verge was an extension brought it to a crashing stop.

Carla woke, damp with perspiration, heart pounding. It took a few moments for her to adjust. That moaning was the wind, not a human being in mortal pain. That rolling motion was the boat, pushed around by the wind, not a car turning over and over.

Some instinct warned that the weather conditions were worsening. An uneasy sleep claimed her and when, in one period of alertness, she heard the pounding of the rain on the trees, on the ground, on the roof over her head, she clutched the bedclothes.

The boat was rocking badly, the wind howling through every crack and entry point. It was gale force now. The conditions grew so alarming, Carla pushed aside the coverings and peered outside, clutching at the other berth for support.

There was a particularly strong gust which the frail, neglected boat could not withstand. The vessel danced and pranced to the gale's wild song, finally breaking free from its mooring. The boat was drifting helplessly to the centre of the river.

Instinct made her pull on a sweater and race up the steps for the steering gear. For agonising moments she struggled with the motor, then it fired and she was able to steer, although the gale's strength was such that it became useless to guide the floundering boat. To Carla's dismay, the motor cut out. Panic rose, but she stayed at the wheel. Conquering the hysteria that threatened, she tried to ease the boat towards the opposite bank. Other boats were in the way and she was terrified at the possibility of a collision.

The roar of the weir reminded her of its drawing power. If she didn't keep away from that . . . Then she remembered the white house. It possessed its own private mooring. Surely, in the circumstances, she would be allowed by whoever was in residence at the house to stay there for the rest of the night?

The weir's sound, swollen by the rain, grew deafening. Wet through, her hair whipped into her eyes and she scraped at it frantically. Her soaked clothes clung, hanging heavily. If only the boat had carried a life-jacket! She had searched for one the day before without success.

There was an alarming pull beneath the hull. If she did not correct the boat's direction . . . After four attempts, the motor restarted. Using all her strength, she was able to wrench the vessel away from the weir and from certain disaster.

There in front of her the great white house

loomed. As the boat bumped alongside the private mooring, Carla jumped on to the duckboards and grabbed the rope which had been trailing in the water.

This time she hoped the knot she made would hold. Patricia's brother Derrick had tried to teach her the rudiments of knot-tying, but in the panic of the moment she had forgotten every word. Returning to the boat, she attempted to dry her hair. Her sweater was soaked and she shivered as she removed it. Even when she had replaced it with a dry one, her body kept on shaking.

Her wet slacks still clung, her shirt too, but she could not find another. Once again she lay on the bunk, but the blankets did not warm her. All the time there was the threatening roar of the weir, and there was no more sleep in her to shut it out.

Only when a grey dawn broke did she sink into a deep, unreviving sleep. She even woke up shivering. It took a few moments for her to realise that it was a shout that had awakened her.

'What the hell do you think you're doing,' the angry male demanded, 'making use of a private mooring? Will you get out from there?'

Carla crawled from the berth and made her way up the steps to the open air. The wind whipped her still-damp hair across her eyes. It pierced the clammy covering of her clothes and the shaking grew worse.

Her pale face lifted to the tall figure of a man standing at the edge of the lawn, and she caught her breath. His hands were in his pockets, his legs held stiffly and belligerently apart. His head was arrogantly high, braving the gale. There was her answer.

Blaze Douglas, owner of the great white riverside house, was at home after all.

It was vital that he did not see her face, although, she reasoned, she must have changed so much he probably would not recognise her. After all, he'd only had a glimpse as she had lain, partly conscious, in the hospital bed. Yet whether or not he knew her, he surely wouldn't begrudge her a few hours more of sanctuary, until the storm died down?

Her hands gripped the boat's side as it wallowed in the swell. 'Please,' she implored, allowing the long red-gold strands to cover her face, 'let me stay and ride out the rough weather. I promise I'll move the moment you want to use the mooring.'

The man's expression hardened. 'I'm sorry.' It was a dismissal, not an apology. 'This is private.'

'Look,' she indicated her state, 'I'm soaked through. The boat lets in water, and everything inside is wet. I c-can't stop shivering.'

'Then go home. To your husband, your parents, your boy-friend, or whoever else you live with.'

'I can't go home. My parents are abroad, and m-my boy-friend's got s-someone else.'

'Don't weep on my shoulder. I'm telling you to get out.'

For a long moment their eyes held. In his she saw no weakening, no pity. After all that Crispin had told her about him, how could she have expected otherwise? Her eyes dropped and closed. Her grip on the boat tightened as she fought the emotions which were rocking her memory as the boat rocked her body.

At last she said, 'Please will you untie the rope?'

nothing she could do to reclaim the makeshift mooring. Now she would have to look for another resting
place. The prospect daunted her.

If she had felt better, maybe she would have been
equal to the problem. If she had been able to cook
herself a meal, her strength would have carried her
through. As it was, all she could do was to cruise up
and down the river, searching endlessly and in vain.

An hour and a half later it was almost dark. Carla
had not found a single piece of bank against which
the boat could nestle. Did it mean that she was
doomed to cruise all night up and down the river?
Then she realised the fuel supply would have run
out long before then.

Blaze Douglas's house was the only answer. As
soon as it was dark she would creep back and moor
her boat. If he came out again she would plead,
play on his pity—she knew he had no compassion—
tell him that in the morning she would go. Those
people who had taken her piece of bank could not
stay there for ever.

Storm clouds brought an early darkness, and the
boat started to rock again. The rain poured down,
the river hurled itself over the weir and the noise, in
her unhappy state of mind, seeming almost to
beckon, caused the shivering to start again.

Cutting the motor, Carla guided the boat until it
bumped against the wooden boards of the mooring.
Keeping her head down, she made her way to the
post and tied the rope as quickly as she could.

Stepping back into the boat, she found a saucepan
and tins of food, and heated them on the camping
stove. The hot meal filled the nagging void inside
her and the coffee she drank warmed her through.

Having more energy set her brain functioning and it proceeded to present her with the inescapable facts of her situation.

She had no right to be where she was, yet she could not go where, for nearly a month, she had managed to hide. If Blaze Douglas chose again to order her away, the law would be on his side. Then where would she go? Fearfully she listened to the weir. Would that be her destiny?

Putting a hand to her head, she slumped on to the bunk. I'm getting lightheaded, she told herself, then felt her forehead with the back of her hand. Her skin was burning and she thought she might have a temperature. There was a howl of wind and it swept through the boat. The shivering started again.

Carla lay on the bunk, covering herself, but the shaking persisted. Tears of desperation rose, but she dashed them away. This was not the time to be weak. She had to think . . . The trouble was that her brain was clouding over again. The energy the meal had given her had been used up and weakness threatened.

Her dream was turning into a nightmare and she woke to find the boat dipping and rising even more perilously than the night before. There seemed to be a sharp tug making the boat swing to one side. Blaze Douglas was back . . . He was setting her adrift . . . Throwing off the covers, she forced herself up the steps to find a man bending over the mooring post.

'No!' she shrieked, and her voice was lifted and played with by the wind. 'Have some pity. Let me stay, just till morning . . .' The man straightened. It was not Blaze Douglas but an older, stouter man wearing a raincoat.

'Listen, madam,' he shouted, cupping his hands, 'I'm obeying Mr Douglas's orders.'

'P-please ask him . . . for me. Just a few hours. If I can't stay here, I don't know what I'll do. I'll d-die. I'm ill, tell him I'm ill.'

'You're too young to die.' The words were shouted by a taller man who appeared from the darkness.

Carla ignored his sarcasm and cried out. 'Have you lost all your feelings? Can't you recognise someone who's really in distress? I need somewhere to stay for a few hours—just a few hours.' The words tailed off hopelessly.

'Mr Douglas?' the man asked. 'What shall I do?'

'Just let me stay here till morning,' Carla shrieked over the rising gale. 'The weir——' she pointed, 'I'm terrified of the weir. The boat's leaking, I'm standing in water . . .'

Blaze Douglas was on the duckboards in a few strides. He went on to his haunches and gripped the hull, working the boat up and down. He's freeing it, Carla thought, he's going to push me out to the current that flows to the weir.

'No!' she shouted. 'Please no!' She bent down to grip the boards, found a hold and fastened her fingers on to it. In doing so, she tipped the boat and it began to move away, taking her feet with it. Her rubber-soled shoes slipped and she fell forward, banging her ribs on the boat's side. She cried out in agony and, robbed of breath, slumped, her hands trailing in the water, her hair hanging down and trailing it, too.

Helpless now, she lay exhausted, each gasping breath hurting, every part of her throbbing with pain. She was being dragged free, her hips, her thighs, her legs, all scraping on an edge.

Arms were lifting her, carrying her, her head lolled on to a shoulder so comforting, she could have stayed there for ever.

CHAPTER TWO

THERE was movement as if she was being carried upstairs. A soft bed gave beneath her and it was bliss. Voices floated around her.

'Herbert, get Ellen, will you? The girl needs clean clothes, a thorough wash.'

'I'm sorry,' Carla found herself mumbling, 'to put you to so much trouble.' There was no answer. 'I tried to keep clean.' Her eyelids were too heavy to lift them. 'My things on the boat . . .' She turned her head from side to side.

A man's voice said, 'They're soaking wet, Mr Douglas. It's taking in water.'

'The boat's not mine. What shall I do?' Her voice sounded strange and thin.

'Try and get some help to haul it out, Herbert. See if Rolf Horner's around. If he's in bed, get him out of it—he won't mind. He'd do anything to rescue a boat in distress.'

'Mr Douglas?' It was a woman's voice now. 'A young lady? Oh, my goodness! I'll get water. Clothes, you said. Do you think Miss Janetta's will fit her?'

'I think they'll hang like a sack, Ellen, but does it matter?'

'She looks flushed, Mr Douglas.'

The back of a hand touched Carla's forehead gently. 'A temperature, I'd guess.'

Her limbs ached, her ribs throbbed, her head burned. Her lips were parched and she tried to moisten them with a dry tongue. Her eyes fluttered open and there was a face gazing down, brows pleated, eyes working at a puzzle they were determined to solve.

'Call the doctor, Ellen,' said Blaze Douglas. The face staring broodingly at her hinted at an inflexibility about which Crispin had once informed her. 'He'll be against our marriage,' he'd said.

'Please don't bother any doctor,' Carla whispered. 'I'll get better with time. But time is something I haven't got.' Her mind must have seemed to onlookers to be wandering. They could not know that what she had said was true. She couldn't stay here pretending she did not know the man who had rescued her when, three years ago, she had been engaged to his brother.

'Go ahead, Ellen.' The imperious instruction sent the woman on her way.

Carla closed her eyes again and her head twisted restlessly. 'I told you, I don't need a doctor.'

A hand touched her forehead, this time smoothing back her hair. 'What's your name?'

She stiffened, forcing her brain to function. If she told him the truth, she would be taking a risk. Crispin might once have mentioned her name unguardedly.

'C-Carol—Carol Smith.'

'I see.' The answer was toneless. She dared not meet his eyes. 'Where do you live, Miss Smith?'

'On the boat.' Now she searched his face in the dimmed lighting of the bedroom. 'I did tell you.'

'You also told me you were a down-and-out, not to mention human driftwood. I didn't believe that, either.'

'Perhaps I'd better tell you again. I'm unemployed, I'm homeless, and I have very little money.'

'And your boy-friend, with whom you lived, has deserted you.'

'I never said that.'

'He found someone else, you said.'

'Oh, will you leave me alone!' She rolled on to her side away from him and pulled the pillow around her head.

'Mr Douglas,' Ellen had returned, 'I'm going to wash the young lady. Will you please go out?'

Blaze Douglas moved to the door.

'Ever washed a piece of human driftwood before, Ellen? Well, you're about to do so now.'

'She's nothing of the sort, Mr Douglas! She's a well-spoken young lady whom the world has treated harshly. It must have done, judging by her thinness—not to mention the way she seems to have been living.'

'Good background, would you say, Ellen? Not rich, but certainly not poor? Attractive, maybe, when she was young?'

'Goodness gracious, Mr Douglas,' the woman reprimanded, 'she's still young. Untouched, I'd say.'

'Would you, Ellen?' There was a derisive note which Carla heard although, with her eyes shut tightly, she did not see the speaker's face. 'Even in these days when girls surrender their innocence to the first man who tries to take it from them? Or so they say?'

'Mr Douglas, this water's getting cold. I'm not going to wash a feverish, half-starved young woman in cold water.'

'I'm taking the hint, Ellen. By the way, she tells me her name is Carol Smith.' Carla had not enough strength to counter the sarcasm so her eyes stayed closed.

It seemed he paused at the door. 'Is Herbert dealing with the boat?'

'Mr Horner got out of his bed to give a hand, Mr Douglas. He said he didn't mind at all.'

Ellen was gentle with her washing, then she helped Carla into a filmy blue nightgown. 'Sorry, Miss Smith, but it's all I could find. Miss Janetta—she's Mr Horner's sister—loves frilly, frothy things.'

'Does she live here, Mrs——?'

'Call me Ellen, dear. I'm Mr Douglas's housekeeper. Herbert's my husband. He gives a hand wherever one's needed. No, Miss Janetta doesn't live here.' Ellen pulled the bedclothes over Carla. 'She lives in London, really. The house farther along the river belongs to Mr Rolf. He's away a lot, too. He works for a firm in the same line as Mr Douglas. Well, whenever Miss Janetta comes down and her brother's away, she can't stand being at the house alone.'

'So she stays here? Which is why some of her clothes are here?'

Ellen nodded.

'And Mr Douglas doesn't mind?'

'Not at all, dear, not at all.' Her tone was bland,

her hands over-busy. 'I can hear the doctor coming.
Now you're nice and clean, you look a different
girl.'

'I'm thirsty, Ellen.'

'When the doctor's gone, I'll give you a little
drink.' The doctor entered, followed by Blaze. Ellen
stepped into the background.

Blaze swung the door without closing it. He stayed
there, arms folded, eyes half closed. The doctor's
practised glance took in Carla's feverish state, the
tiny tremors which, despite the warm bedclothes,
periodically racked her body.

'I hear you've been living somewhat dangerously,
young woman,' the doctor remarked, smiling pater-
nally. 'However, you seem to have survived—
how well, we shall have to investigate. Your name
is——?'

Carla spoke her assumed name so quietly, the
doctor was forced to bend down. A voice behind
him gave the information he sought. 'Carla
Howard.'

The doctor did not see the negative shake of her
head. 'It's——'

'Unless,' Blaze Douglas persisted, 'in the three
years since I saw her, she's acquired—and shed—a
husband?'

'So you know her, Blaze,' the doctor commented.

Ellen, in the shadows, made a startled movement.

'Know of her might be more accurate. About the
time my brother died.'

A finger rested gently on Carla's pulse, and the
doctor's frown indicated guarded surprise at its
accelerating rate. The thermometer in her mouth
prevented her from making any explanation. So

Blaze Douglas was aware of her real identity! What should she do? More important, what would he do to her? But she was blameless, surely he knew that. The thermometer was removed, studied, shaken and put away. A palm tested the burning forehead, fingers probed her neck glands.

'I should like to examine you, Miss Howard. Ellen——?'

The housekeeper approached, helping Carla to sit up. Anxiously Carla sought out Blaze, discovering to her relief that he had gone.

She winced at the doctor's exploratory touch on her ribs, making him ask, 'You hurt here?'

Carla nodded. 'When Mr—Mr Douglas pulled me out of the boat, my ribs hit against the side.' That was not the whole truth, and she guessed the doctor knew it. 'Three years ago I was involved in a car accident,' she explained. 'I finished up in hospital with fractured ribs and a dislocated shoulder, plus some concussion. Crispin, Mr Douglas's brother,' her voice dropped to a whisper, 'was thrown out, but his injuries were so bad he only lived for an hour or two. But I expect you know that.'

Ellen went out in answer to a call.

There was a long pause, then the doctor nodded. 'You must calm down, Miss Howard. In your state you need rest, not agitation.'

Carla smiled weakly.

'Your ribs healed completely and without trouble three years ago, I assume?' the doctor asked, rising. Carla nodded. 'Your shoulder, too? Good. Well, this recent escapade has unfortunately bruised your ribs again, but time will heal them, as it will cure your other infection. But you must rest. That's the best cure, in the present circumstances. I'll give you pills for the throat. For the bruising, you must stay in bed for a couple of days at least. You do understand?'

There was a tap at the door and Ellen returned. The doctor wrote on his pad, giving the prescription to her. She made Carla comfortable and as she went away, Blaze came to stand in the doorway, and the doctor repeated to him the advice he had given to Carla. 'Miss Howard understands how important it is that she should rest completely for a couple of days at least,' he told Blaze.

'I don't know how I can do that, doctor,' Carla interrupted urgently. 'The only home I've got is the boat.'

'Which,' said Blaze, entering, 'is unusable.'

'Then I'll just have to take my chance and leave here, find a room——'

'With no money?' Blaze's voice was dismissing. 'You'll have to stay here.'

'That would be the best arrangement,' the doctor confirmed.

'How can I——?'

'Miss Howard, if you leave here in your present state,' the doctor told her firmly, 'I take no responsibility for the outcome. You have my professional advice. I trust you'll be sensible enough to take it.'

Carla nodded, thanked him and turned her cheek to the pillow. When she opened her eyes moments later she found she was alone with Blaze. His gaze was intense and, to her sensitive gaze, faintly accusing.

'You didn't have to take responsibility for me,'

she felt impelled to say. 'I told you I only wanted to tie up my boat at your mooring for the night. Yet you——' her voice wavered, 'you actually tried to push me away, right into the path of the weir! I was frightened out of my wits by the weir—I *told* you.' She had to stop before her throat thickened with tears. She wished he would speak, say something, anything to establish contact.

Her gaze wandered and for the first time she noticed the room's furnishings. It was neat, clean and, from the feel of it, unused. There was not a feminine touch about it.

'Whose room am I using, Mr Douglas?' she asked.

He stood, hands cupping elbows, dark shadows round his chin and cheeks, a forbidding, inflexible figure. So younger brother had not invented the tale of older brother's hardness. 'You should know, Miss Howard. Or has time robbed you of all recollection of the happy times you spent here with Crispin?'

'It's Crispin's room?'

'It was. I thought you might find its familiarity reassuring.'

Carla said dully, turning her face away, 'I didn't spend any "happy times" here with Crispin.'

'Why, was he such a bad lover?'

She would not tell this insolent man the truth! Her burning, hate-filled eyes met his. 'Do you really think I'd tell you if he was or not?'

'Knowing the kind of person you were,' he came back relentlessly, 'no, I wouldn't.'

Her head turned away again. She was in no condition to do battle with him. Yet even in her weakened condition she could feel the tug of his physical attraction, his dark, handsome features, his lean, long body, as strongly as she had felt the tug of the weir.

One thing she knew. Never, she resolved, would she become involved with him, never go over the top and flounder in the multi-currents of emotion she sensed he could arouse within any woman he chose. For if she ever did, she knew without doubt that she would drown in him, never again to surface.

Morning brought Carla an unfamiliar sensation of peace, and her ears concentrated on listening to her surroundings. Over the past month it was a habit she had developed, on waking from a rocking sleep on a hard cabin cruiser berth.

Although she was safe—in a bed, in a house, on dry land—her mind pushed through the half-opened window and performed its customary function of taking soundings of the immediate environment. The trees and the undergrowth might, in the night, have turned into a jungle. Every rustle could have heralded a lurking predator—or some Council official come to order her to move on.

Heard from a distance, the sounds were different— yet the same. There was still the unceasing tumble of the weir, the faint lap of river against bank, the bark of an excited dog. Then, from somewhere in the house, came the whine of a vacuum cleaner, bringing her back to reality.

Voices from outside wafted up. 'Blaze, this boat's a shocker! Whoever you pulled out of it can count himself lucky he's alive.'

'For "he" substitute "she", Rolf,' Blaze called back. 'Like the boat's name, a "river lady". Although

I do believe,' his voice was dry now, 'she calls herself less complimentary things. For instance, "scum of the river", and "human driftwood"!'

It's almost as if he knows I can hear, Carla fretted.

'You're joking,' the man called Rolf answered. 'A woman living in this tub? Gipsy type, maybe? Free with her favours? Is that why you rescued her?'

Carla stiffened at the innuendo.

'Gipsy type?' Blaze was speaking again. 'Not really a fitting description. And did you say *free* with her favours?' There was a short, sardonic laugh.

'You don't mean she emptied your pockets? But looking at this rotting wood, I couldn't blame her if she did.'

The blush on Carla's pale cheeks deepened with anger. I'll get out of bed, she thought, go to the window and . . . She scraped together the strength to swing her legs to the floor, but they crumpled beneath her. Turning her face to the bedclothes, she let the tears of frustration run down.

A few minutes later Ellen found her. 'Mr Douglas, Mr Douglas!' the housekeeper called from the door. 'Miss Howard's all in a heap. She must have tried——'

'For God's sake, Carla!' Blaze was there in a few strides. 'What were you trying to do—make a get-away?'

His arms were lifting her and in spite of her weakness, her pulses leapt. He lowered her to the bed, standing silently while Ellen covered her, tucking her in securely.

'Whatever were you doing, Miss Howard?' the housekeeper asked. 'If I hadn't come in then, you could have caught your death. Mr Douglas, shall I call the doctor? Do you think she's feverish, or walking in her sleep?'

Blaze had been regarding her broodingly. His hand tested her forehead. 'I'd guess her temperature was normal. Don't bother the doctor. Were you walking in your sleep, Miss Howard?' His eyebrow lifted quizzically.

'I was wide awake, Mr Douglas. It was my *hearing* that was troubling me. Words like "gipsy type" and "free with her favours" and emptying your pockets.' Her angry brown eyes fought a battle with his, but her mouth couldn't fight his sardonic smile. 'I wanted to shout the truth from the window, put the record straight in the mind of that man you were talking to. But I couldn't make it.'

'It's your illness, dear,' Ellen comforted, misunderstanding, 'it often makes your ears go funny. Isn't that true, Mr Douglas?'

'Oh, very true, Ellen.' Amusement curved Blaze's hard mouth, narrowed his grey eyes. 'Carla, do you want breakfast?'

The housekeeper broke in, 'A nice boiled egg, dear? Something on toast?'

Carla shook her head. 'I wouldn't mind some fruit, like——'

'Grapefruit, Miss Howard,' Ellen suggested, 'all nicely cut, with sugar sprinkled on it and a cherry on top?'

Carla nodded eagerly. 'And tea, Ellen, not coffee?' Ellen was away before Carla had finished talking.

'Simple tastes,' Blaze commented, his hands thrust into his fawn slacks pockets, his dark-red shirt open at the neck.

'Acquired through necessity,' she responded shortly. Her head turned away. 'Sorry, I mustn't weep on your shoulder. Your instructions, shouted to me over the top of a howling gale the night before last.'

'If you'd told me you were the ex-fiancée of my late brother, instead of hiding your identity under layers of that hair——' His eyes narrowed again. 'Incidentally, why did you try to disguise yourself?'

Her head stayed turned away.

'Of course, I get it now. Crispin must have told you how strongly I opposed his engagement to you.'

'He did tell me,' she answered tiredly. 'He also said that since your parents split up and eventually married other partners, you'd become overbearing and dictatorial towards him.'

'I was eight years older than Crispin. In the absence of any guidance from our parents, what did you expect me to do when I saw him tying himself to a girl who was completely unsuited to him? Stand on the sidelines and cheer?'

She could not let that pass unchallenged. 'What do you mean, "unsuited to him"? If you mean "socially unacceptable", why don't you say so? I was too low down the social scale, maybe?'

'You want to know?' The look in his eyes hinted at the verbal onslaught to come. 'Too young, too stupid, too shallow. The exact opposite, in fact, of what he needed.'

'Such as——?'

'A stabilising influence, someone with greater maturity to make up for his lack of it, with common sense and, most of all, tolerance of his occasional lapses of morality.'

'A mother figure, in fact. How he would have appreciated the stolid, unexciting, milk-and-water creature you describe!'

'That "milk-and-water creature" would have stopped him from drinking too much, thereby saving his life.'

'Are you trying to make me feel guilty?' she demanded.

'You were driving. Shouldn't you feel guilty?'

Her head lifted from the pillow, only to drop again. 'You really are blaming me! How do you know I was driving?'

'I saw with my own eyes as you left the party.'

'But we changed over soon after that. Crispin insisted.' Her eyes opened wide. 'You're shaking your head? I tell you we swopped places.'

'The police rang me, and I reached the scene of the accident very quickly. They'd got you both out on the grass verge, and Crispin whispered to me that you were driving.'

Crispin had lied to his brother! It was all so untrue, yet so feasible she could find no way of defending herself.

Blaze Douglas frowned, looking at her with speculation. 'Yet a witness to the accident said he could have sworn that a man was driving.'

Carla's eyes slid to Blaze. 'That bears out my statement that we changed places. Why don't you believe me when I tell you it was Crispin's fault?'

'Even if I did believe you, it wouldn't absolve you from blame. You see,' he came to stand beside the bed, 'the same witness also swore that the woman passenger was distracting the driver so badly—by attempting to put her arms round him and nuzzling up to him—that he wasn't surprised there was an accident.'

Carla's shaking hands lifted to her white cheeks. 'It wasn't true,' she whispered. 'I was pleading with him to be more careful.' Despair dilated her eyes. 'I can see you don't believe me. You'll never believe me!'

There was a knock at the door and a smiling Ellen entered. 'Here we are, Miss Howard—Oh, my dear,' she put down the tray and hurried to the bedside, 'you're shaking! Whatever have you done to make her like that, Mr Douglas?'

Motherly arms lifted Carla and cradled her, and Carla turned gratefully to hide her face in the housekeeper's ample shape. A voice called and Ellen answered, 'Can't it wait, Herbert? Oh, I'll come.' She started to lower Carla to the pillow, but other arms went round the limp form. Ellen said, 'There, Miss Howard, Mr Douglas will comfort you. I won't be more than two minutes.'

At first Carla resisted the strong yet curiously tender hold, but her strength was not equal to that of the man who pulled her to him. The shaking persisted, and only Carla knew it was not entirely caused by her despairing state of mind.

Capitulating to the strange solace offered by her adversary, she let her head rest against the vibrating wall of his chest, found the steady throb of the heartbeat beneath her ear immensely tranquillising, offering a security which, in recent years, she had forgotten existed.

Quiet now, another sensation crept through. It was a feeling more disturbing and far more unsettling than this man's devastating allegations could ever arouse. That the mere contact of his skin against hers could stir her desires so strongly worried her deeply.

'I'm all right now, thank you.' Her voice was small.

He lowered her to the pillow and watched the colour creep into her cheeks. Ellen's busy feet brought her into the room. She picked up the tray and carried it to the bed.

'You're looking better now, Miss Howard.' Her smile was like a piece of the sunshine outside brought into the room. 'Mr Douglas must have the magic touch. He's cured you better than the doctor! Now, Mr Douglas, could you just help the patient to sit up so she can eat her breakfast? I'd do it myself, but ——' Her nod indicated the tray.

'Any objections, Carla?' Blaze asked. 'If so, they're overruled.' He smiled ironically. His hands were on her again, this time under the armpits, helping her up. The shiver was at his touch, but Ellen could not read her thoughts.

'You're cold, and no wonder, having to wear that flimsy thing of Miss Janetta's. A bedjacket, Miss Howard—would you mind wearing one of mine? Here's your breakfast.'

While the housekeeper went to find the bedjacket, Carla inspected the tray's contents. 'I can't eat all this, Ellen,' she asserted when the housekeeper returned. 'I said grapefruit and——'

'You couldn't keep a mouse alive on what you said, Miss Howard,' Ellen answered, putting the jacket round Carla's shoulders. 'So I added an egg and toast and——'

'I—I'll do my best, Ellen, but you see, I'm not used to a lot of food all at once. I had to eat sparingly because I couldn't——' She glanced at Blaze, hating to admit in front of him just how short of money she had been.

It seemed he had guessed. 'She was going to say she couldn't afford to eat properly, Ellen.'

At the door, Ellen said, 'Then it's a good thing she was washed up on your doorstep, Mr Douglas.' To Carla, she added, 'Call me when you've finished, dear, and I'll clear away.'

For a few moments Carla stared at the food. 'All this,' she murmured, half to herself, 'it confuses me somehow. It's like a feast. I hardly know where to begin.'

'I'd start with the grapefruit, if I were you,' his dry voice advised.

'Oh, yes,' she answered, with a touch of sarcasm. 'I'd forgotten the social niceties like eating a meal in the correct order.' Her shadowed eyes found his grey gaze. 'It's surprising how quickly abject poverty strips away the layers of conformity imposed by society.'

His expression hardened. 'I'm not quite sure what you're trying to say. That *I* should feel guilty because I turned you away from my private mooring?'

'That, plus the fact that, in your opinion, I wasn't "good enough" for your late brother.' His jawline grew angular and she knew she had goaded him. Her sense of fairness told her she was in the wrong. 'I'm sorry.' She picked up the spoon, digging it into the sugared fruit. 'After all you've done for me, the sarcasm was out of place.'

He nodded curtly and walked to the window. He could have been absorbed by the river scene, but Carla sensed his thoughts were elsewhere.

Appreciating the silence, she continued to indulge the appetite she did not know she had.

Blaze turned at last, saw her leaning back from an almost empty tray, and resumed his inspection of the view outside. 'Tell me something,' he said, 'just why have you spent every evening for the past month standing across the river on the towpath staring at my house?'

'You saw?' she responded, aghast, then injected scorn into her voice. 'Using binoculars, of course.'

'I saw. Without binoculars.' A pause, then, 'Your hair colour is very—distinctive.'

Involuntarily she touched it, trying to think of a suitable answer. Tell him that all through her ordeal after the accident, it was his face, his voice that haunted her, not Crispin's? That she had never forgotten him even though three years had passed since the one and only time they had met?

She recalled how avidly she had read about the enormous international success of his business equipment company and how he had chosen this area of all others to build his world headquarters. She even remembered the date he had moved permanently into this house—after his parents had lost all interest in it—this beautiful house overlooking the River Thames.

Seeing his growing impatience, she answered, 'Haven't you ever heard how the "have-nots" gaze with longing at the possessions of the "haves"? How the poor seek escape in staring at the privileged?' They were half-truths that she had spoken, but she hoped he had been convinced.

He returned to the bedside, putting the tray on a stool. Again he stared down at her. 'You look ill and undernourished. And there's an underlying sadness somewhere. Who caused it, the boy-friend who left you?'

If she told him she had never let a single boy-friend go beyond the barriers she had built around her emotions, would he believe her? Aloud she said, 'Wouldn't anyone look ill and sad if they were homeless and without an income?'

'When you worked, what did you do?'

Carla explained about the small electrical components store she had worked in and how its owner had retired from business and closed the shop all in one day.

'Then my brother wanted my room. The house is his. The woman he'd been living with became pregnant, so they planned on marrying quickly and making my room into a nursery.'

'So they turned you out?'

Carla nodded. 'I couldn't find a place to live in at a rent I could afford, so I borrowed a friend's brother's boat. You can guess the rest.'

'Standard of living touched rock bottom, followed by poverty, deprivation?'

Carla nodded. 'Loss of self-respect.' She stared at the man Crispin had called heartless and without pity. Had Crispin's opinion on the subject been purely brotherly? Did this man possess compassion, after all? His next words answered her questions.

'Life having its revenge for what you did to my brother.' His hooded eyes noticed, with a cruel satisfaction, the draining of her cheeks, the clenching of her fists.

'What *I* did to your brother? Don't you understand? I was not driving! Nor was I pestering him while he drove, like that witness said.'

'Finished with your tray, Miss Howard?' Ellen enquired, entering. 'I knew you'd manage more than you said. And you look a lot better for it—except I wish you had more colour in your cheeks.' She laughed. 'Mr Douglas will have to cuddle you again. That did the trick last time!'

'No, thank you,' Carla answered emphatically, but Ellen had gone.

'Don't worry,' Blaze drawled, 'it's not usually my line to hold a down-and-out of the river world in my arms.'

'You haven't got a kindly, humane bone in your body, have you?' she hit out.

'No, I haven't. Certainly not towards the person who helped my brother to an early grave.'

The shaking began again, her breathing became shallow. 'Why, you——' Pushing aside the bed-clothes, she swung her feet to the floor. With all the strength of her will she forced them to support her.

The four paces to reach him were like a treadmill, but she got to him, raised her fists to his chest, then, as he stood, arms folded, watching, she collapsed against him, sobbing.

CHAPTER THREE

HER cheek was against his chest, her hands clinging to his upper arms. The muscles moved, tensed, and were still. Her control gained a hold and the sobs became less frequent, dying away at last.

There was a movement of her hair, as though an unexpected breeze had stirred it. Fingertips probed and lifted a lock of red-gold hair, then let it fall, and a frisson of pleasure shivered through her. Slowly her head lifted and she sought his face to discern his expression.

The grey eyes were half closed, the square, stubborn chin led to unsmiling lips. A swift movement and she was in his arms, being lowered to the bed. He covered her with the bedclothes as disinterestedly as a medical man, then moved a pace or two away.

Her eyes reached out to him as supplicatingly as her arms would have done had they not been so weakened, like the rest of her, by her illness. Believe me, please, her eyes said, accept what I say as the truth. There was not a spark of response from him and she lowered her lids to shut him out.

'Miss Howard?' The doctor entered. 'Ah, Blaze is with you. You look pale, my dear. Are you tired?'

Carla opened her eyes and managed a smile, but it became a frown. 'Dr Macmillan,' she said, 'I can't stay here. I'm sorry, but I'll have to find somewhere——'

'Blaze?' Blaze Douglas turned a mask of a face towards the other man. 'Did you hear what this girl said?' His fingers found her pulse and he frowned.

'I did.'

'She's in an upset state, Blaze.' Blaze folded his arms again. 'What has this man been saying to you, Miss Howard?'

'Shouldn't you ask Miss Howard what she's being saying to me?'

The doctor's sigh was impatient. 'You've a sharp tongue, Blaze.'

'Yes, doctor.'

Dr Macmillan's thin face was lined with years of caring for others. 'When folks are ill, Blaze, they need loving care, comfort, not hard words.'

'Yes, doctor.'

'Cut out the formality, Blaze.' The doctor's thin bony figure gave no hint of his stamina and fitness. 'I've known you since you were a wee boy. I watched you grow, did I not, and I saw you grow up when your parents parted. I know what you're made of, Blaze, but I know your faults.'

Blaze stayed silent.

'When a young woman as bonny as this one tells me she can't stay here, and her pulse is racing as though it's running in the Olympics, I don't need to look far for the cause.'

Carla whispered into the silence, 'So now you know why I must go, doctor.'

'Well, Blaze,' Dr Macmillan questioned, 'what's the answer?'

'She stays. But I make the statement under duress.'

Carla's fury rose like a rocket. Pushing back the bedcovers, she cried, 'I'm going—I'm not staying here to be insulted!'

Dr Macmillan picked up his case. 'If this girl's condition worsens, let me know at once, and I'll get her into hospital. She'll get a warmer welcome there than any you have to offer.' He did not say 'goodbye'.

Carla's feet were brushing the floor again. Blaze strode across and his hands caught her ankles, lifting them on to the bed, yet letting his fingers linger. Each froze, staring, one with blazing eyes, the other coldly returning that stare, then slowly he straightened, an eyebrow lifted. 'Going somewhere?' he asked caustically.

'I'm not staying in the same house as a man who's determined to hold against me for ever something that just isn't true. I wasn't driving, I tell you!' She held his eyes and something compelled her to say, 'Please tell me you believe me!'

For a few moments his impassive gaze roamed her face, then dropped to dwell on the full swell of her breasts which were plainly visible beneath the misty blue of the borrowed gown she was wearing.

'I believe you,' he replied at last, 'but only because the police informed me at the scene of the accident that when they took you both from the wreckage, you appeared to be wearing the passenger seat-belt and my brother was not. In fact, he was completely unprotected. Which, they said, was why his injuries were so bad he died from them a couple of hours later.'

Carla sank back on to the pillow, drawing the bedjacket round her. His words had momentarily jerked open the blinds on the nightmare sequences of the terrible crash. A few moments later she rallied, and hit back.

'Thank you for your faith in my honesty, grudging though it is!'

At once she became aware of the fact that her sarcastic statement formed a challenge. If Blaze felt inclined to accept it as such, she reproached herself, she would be unable to deal with his calculated retaliation.

Her energies had been depleted by her brief struggle with him, not to mention the acid exchanges with the man, who seemed to take increasing delight in harassing her. Until she regained her strength she would, verbally, have to tread lightly. Once again she turned from him, pulling the covers over her and closing her eyes to exclude him from her sight and her thoughts.

It did not take her long to realise, however, that it would have been easier to have denied the existence of the roaring weir while drifting towards it in a rudderless boat. The softness of his breathing, his very stillness pounded on her consciousness like a stick on a primitive drum.

When he went out she had no idea. She had drifted into a troubled sleep.

When she opened her eyes again, it was evening. The sun's rays slanted through the wide windows, the curtains filled with the gentle breeze and emptied again.

Carla thought she was alone until she focused her sleep-lazy eyes and saw the tall figure gazing out, his back broad, his leg muscles easy with a thoughtful relaxation. His hands were pocketed, his head turned slightly, revealing an enigmatic profile.

'Blaze?' Carla whispered, wisps of her dreams softening the remote outline at the window.

'Yes?' The word came colourlessly, as if he already knew of her wakefulness.

'I'm not enjoying being a trouble to you, even if you think I am.'

He did not answer for a long time. Carla lay, as still as he was, watching him. When he spoke at last, what he had to say started her adrenalin pumping.

'Was it my brother's money you were after?'

Colour stained her pale cheeks. Would this man never stop attacking her?

He turned slowly, leaning back against the sill, arms folded. 'One of the first things I noticed about you as you lay on the grass verge was the ruby and diamond ring you were wearing. I remember thinking that the expensive and elaborate design went with your youth—and your character.'

'A ruby has colour and warmth. What would go with your character, Mr Douglas?' she threw back. 'A piece of ice, coated with frost? Except that ice melts, whereas you'd never melt even in a burning stream of lava!'

He contemplated coolly her sparking brown eyes and went on as though she had not spoken, 'What did you do with the ring—sell it and spend the money on luxuries you were denied by the loss of your fiancé?'

'I—I kept it.'

His unfeeling regard unnerved her, making her eyes fall before his. 'If you must know,' she went on, 'I've kept the ring as a kind of financial fallback. If at any time I found myself really penniless—I've been near to it but not quite rock-bottom—I thought I could sell it and use the money to exist on.'

'Exist—that's all you've been doing for the past month, isn't it?'

'Not only for the past month.'

'For the last three years?'

Her gaze swung upwards to meet his challenge. 'No!' How could she tell him, It wasn't Crispin I loved . . .

'How long since the boy-friend deserted?'

'I was never serious with him. It's no good shaking

your head, Mr Douglas. I'm telling you the truth, not fairy stories.' She reached out with her eyes beyond the window panes. If only she were walking freely by the river, away from this inquisition . . . 'I don't even know myself what's been wrong, so how can I tell you? Lack of a stable background, maybe.' She was thinking aloud. 'The feeling that I wasn't really wanted in my brother's house. Who knows?'

Her glance had broken through the confines of the panes of glass. 'I think I was happiest, really, in the past month. Out there on the river, I was free to come and go. I had just enough money to keep my appetite satisfied, buy a second-hand sweater or jeans when I needed them. If only the boat had been sound . . .'

'Your belongings were mostly salvaged from the sinking ship.' There was a mocking note, but she looked up anxiously.

'Did the boat sink?'

'No. I was speaking metaphorically.'

'Sorry,' she responded dully. 'My mental reflexes to jokes and innuendoes aren't working at their normal speed.' Her head sought the comfort of the pillow and her eyes closed. 'I wish they were. It would mean I was back to my usual fitness. Then I could leave.'

'Do you hate it here so much?'

'No, I love it here——'

His gaze mocked as he caught her out. 'So the "have-not" is enjoying her stay in the house of one of the "haves"? You've managed to cross the river from the opposite bank not only mentally, as you did this past month, but physically. Here you are, in the elegant residence of one of the "privileged". I've used your words, Miss Howard.'

Carla slid lower in the bed, pulling the covers to her chin. 'Why are you always hitting out at me, making me feel small?' It was difficult to keep her voice steady. 'You keep putting false constructions on my actions, deliberately misunderstanding my meanings. What have I ever done to you to make you like this towards me?'

He strolled to the bedside and saw the brown, swimming eyes. 'Deprived my brother of his right to live his full life-span?'

'If I tell you again that I didn't cause the accident, you won't believe me. If I say that too much alcohol was to blame, plus his own "spoilt little boy" nature, you wouldn't believe me.'

'Why did he drink too much at the party, Miss Howard?' Her eyes were closed so she felt, before she saw, the hand that pushed back a stray lock of red-gold hair.

Memories of the party drifted back—the way Crispin had sulked after she'd broken the news of her decision to end the engagement, the way he'd said, 'I'm going to get drunk, and you're getting drunk with me'. These were things she could never speak of to this man.

She met his measured gaze and felt like a gale that had suddenly blown itself out. 'Maybe he was thirsty?' she offered tiredly, and closed her eyes.

Life passed by outside in the form of sounds. There were shouts, laughter, a dog growling. Carla wished, with every bone in her strengthening body, that she could join the makers of those sounds. She longed to laugh with them as they skimmed the surface of living instead of plunging headlong in as circumstances had forced her to do.

Ellen came in one morning to collect the breakfast tray. 'Hardly a crumb left,' she approved. 'The doctor's just phoned instead of calling today, and he suggests you sit outside this morning. The sun's warm, the roof of the patio overlooking the garden will keep the breeze off you. What about it, Miss Howard?'

'The thought of it makes me feel better, Ellen! I'm sure I'm a lot stronger now.'

'I've never seen anyone so determined to get her strength back,' Ellen commented with a smile. 'Walking around this room for the last day or so as if you were a caged lion!'

'I think you mean lioness, Ellen.'

The housekeeper laughed. 'I'll ask Herbert to carry you down.' She brushed aside Carla's protests that she could walk down the stairs herself. 'You get dressed, Miss Howard. I've put a few of Miss Janetta's clothes in your wardrobe. You've filled out a bit since you arrived here, so the clothes should fit you better.'

Carla selected black velvet slacks and a long-sleeved cream shirt-blouse which seemed to be made of silk. They were not her own taste, mainly because she had never had sufficient money to buy quality, therefore never wasted time looking at it. She was combing the tangles from her long, curling hair when Ellen returned.

'My goodness, those black trousers fit you fine, Miss Howard. In fact, you look a different girl, out of a different world. You could almost be a model, dear. I wonder what Mr Douglas will think of you when he comes back from London.'

He'll think the same as before, Carla told herself resignedly. He won't see me as I am, but as the girl who, in his opinion, deprived his brother of the right to live.

'I've got a nice comfortable chair ready for you, Miss Howard,' Herbert announced, walking in after knocking. 'My word, you're as light as a feather!' He carried her with ease down the broad, curving staircase.

Carla looked about her, remembering the times she had been there before.

The carpet was as deeply red as it had always been, and of such quality that, even three years later, there were no signs of wear. Yes, quality would surely be the most important thing Blaze Douglas would require in all his possessions, whether inanimate or living and breathing.

Which woman, she wondered, glancing at the ornate and gilded ceiling of the ballroom as they passed through, did he possess at the moment? Something deep inside her stirred restlessly at the idea of his close involvement with any woman.

The sunshine dazzled as Herbert lowered her gently into the lounger he had prepared for her. Even though she protested, he covered her legs with a rug.

'Ellen's orders,' he explained, adding with a smile, 'I never disobey my wife, miss!'

Ellen followed with a wifely comment, and placed a pile of magazines on Carla's lap. Alone, Carla had little desire to read. All she wanted was to watch the sounds she seemed to have heard for half a lifetime up in that bedroom, being translated into movement and visual reality.

Cabin cruisers drifted by, mostly small craft, painted white but with panels of contrasting colours here and there. Their occupants were holiday-makers, dressed for leisure and relaxation. Some of them she recognised from the time she had spent on the *River Lady*. With a strange touch of nostalgia she remembered the boat and for the first time grew concerned over its whereabouts and condition.

Shading her eyes, she looked towards the end of the sloping lawn. There was a boat resting on the paved area that formed the mooring. It was—she was sure it was—the *River Lady*. A head bobbed about inside it and now and then there was the sound of hammering.

The man straightened, absorbed by the work he was doing. His hair was brown, his shape that of a man who denied himself little. Yet he was young, Carla was sure, his movements quick and practised.

As if her regard had touched him, he looked up. The sight of her seemed to intrigue him. He put down his hammer and stepped over the boat's side. His smile as he approached was as broad and welcoming as if she were an old friend. He pulled up a footstool and sat on it, looking up at her.

'My name's Rolf Horner,' he said. 'I know yours.'

Carla nodded in greeting, returning his smile with a tentative one of her own.

'So you're Blaze's own personal piece of flotsam,' he continued. 'I wish the river had washed you up on my doorstep. I wouldn't have thrown you back like Blaze did.'

'You mean send me away? How do you know he did?'

'Gossip, down at the Boat Club. We both belong. So does my sister Janetta, when she's here. You haven't met her yet.' There was a brotherly insinuation there that warned, You don't know what's coming.

Carla laughed. 'I've been wearing her clothes. There was nothing else, and Ellen said your sister wouldn't mind. My things were left in the boat.'

'Is that what the sodden mess was that we found in a locker? You mean those were *clothes*? Janetta would call them rags and chuck them out.'

'Yes, well,' Carla moved the rug away, its weight too warm in the sun, 'obviously her tastes and mine differ. Not to mention her purchasing power.'

'She earns good money, being personal assistant to my boss.'

'You both work for the same company—the one Ellen said was a rival to Blaze's?'

'Yes,' his voice lowered theatrically, 'bitter rivals. Good friends on the surface, but behind our backs, we tear each other's eyes out!'

Carla laughed. There was a pause and she gazed towards the river, feeling, as she did so, his eyes curiously upon her.

'What are you doing to my boat?' she asked. 'Whatever it is, you're working very hard.'

'I'm indulging myself with my favourite hobby— messing about in boats. I'm doing a resuscitation job on it. It's a wonder you didn't drown.'

'My friend's brother—he's the owner—lost interest and left it to rot. That's why he let me have it rent free,' she explained.

'So I'll send the bill to him.' He saw her frown. 'I didn't mean it, Carla. I wouldn't charge someone like you.' His voice had softened. Carla felt flattered but otherwise unmoved. No man, she realised with a stab of fear, could ever stir her emotions and her secret longings like Blaze ... But why does that frighten me? she wondered. Is it because I know that he'll never return my love? *Love*? I *love* him?

Rolf was looking at her legs, outlined by the black slacks, at the hips and slim waist they clung to. He glanced at the white hand lying on her thigh and looked as if he would like to take the hand in his. Instead he commented, 'My sister's clothes fit you well.'

Carla thanked him, feeling an unexpected strain between them.

'When you're completely recovered, we must go out somewhere, a meal, or dancing.'

'It's a kind thought, Rolf, but,' Carla frowned, 'I can't stay here indefinitely. I've got no claim on Blaze's hospitality——'

'You were engaged to his brother Crispin, or so Blaze told me. Doesn't that make you—almost—one of the family?'

Carla coloured, wondering if the remark was prompted by the belief that everyone seemed to hold that she and Crispin had been lovers. 'Not at all,' she denied. 'As soon as I'm able, I must move on——'

'Going so soon?' The voice came from behind her and Rolf's eyes lifted to look past her at the speaker. 'Leave us your address, will you, Miss Howard? Ellen might like to keep in touch. She's taking such a motherly interest.'

Blaze Douglas moved to stand beside the lounger, his arms folded, eyes in shadow, gazing at the fiery head of hair resting back against the cushions.

'Ouch,' Rolf remarked, rising from the stool, 'such shafts of sarcasm, Blaze. Enough to draw blood from the flawless skin of your very own "river lady"!'

'Spoken like a true salesman, Rolf. Where does your poetry come from? It's not in the technical literature you distribute amongst your would-be customers.'

'Beginning to wish I was on your side, Blaze? Your friend and employee and not your sworn business enemy?'

'If I were, Rolf, I'd have made you a financial offer long ago that you couldn't refuse.'

'Ouch again!' His smile was broad, his eyes laughing. 'I melt away. Exit one unwelcome guest, into the bowels of the boat at the bottom of Blaze's garden.' Rolf glanced at Carla. 'I'm making good progress, but it may take some while to get her completely riverworthy. Okay?'

'It's very good of you, Rolf.'

'Don't mention it. I'll send the bill to Old Father Thames himself.'

Carla laughed, the young man's charm touching a curiously responsive chord within her. The silence that followed lasted so long that Carla felt impelled to break it. 'Rolf seems to know about boats.'

Blaze moved to occupy the footstool which Rolf had vacated. He, however, sat with his back to her. Carla did not take offence. Instead she smiled. Blaze Douglas, she reflected, was not the kind of man to gaze up adoringly into any woman's face.

'Rolf Horner's been mad about boats since he sat surrounded by the plastic variety as a baby in the bathtub. Or so his sister says.'

There was a pause, and the sound of hammering started again. 'As the years passed—again this came from Janetta,' Blaze continued, 'he went through the usual stages, progressing eventually to a cabin cruiser, and then a yacht of his own. What he doesn't know about things that float hasn't been invented.'

'Does he really mean he won't want paying? He jokes about it——'

'It's no joke on his part. He's enjoying himself. Just forget it.'

'Thanks for the advice. But I——' Carla wished her powers of communication were as skilful as Rolf Horner's, but then she never was much good at selling anything, not even herself. Mr Hulton, her recent employer, had discovered this soon after she had gone to work for him. He had found a use for her better-than-average powers of adding and subtracting in the small, untidy office adjoining the shop. 'I can't go on living here without——'

'What was it you were saying about moving on?' Blaze interrupted smoothly. He stood, pushing the footstool away impatiently with his foot. 'Have you heard from your brother while I've been absent, offering you a room at his house?'

'No. I just——'

'Maybe you've seen an advertisement in the local paper for a rented flat?'

'No, again. I——'

'Or have you decided to spend the rest of your life wandering, pack on your back, moving from one youth hostel to another?'

'No, I have not!' she retorted, her fingers tight around the lounger's armrests. 'But I know one thing—I can't stay here.'

'My offer of a roof over your head extended beyond your recovery from your illness.' He looked down at her, his eyes skimming her reclining body. When Rolf had looked at her like that, her reaction had been nil. This man's very male scrutiny aroused her indignation and something far more primitive. She bristled at the audacity of his roaming eyes, and grew angry, both with him and herself, for allowing her heart to pound so painfully, and her dulled emotions to be so disturbed.

He had no right to have such an effect on her. All the accusations Crispin had made about him came back to her mind—inflexible, autocratic, unscrupulous, he'd called him. Yes, he had been right—this man was all these things. She had seen that for herself now.

'There's no need for you to feel under any obligation to befriend me, Mr Douglas,' Carla said distantly. 'I deprived your brother of his life, remember?'

His eyes narrowed. 'Now use your logic, Miss Howard. How could a man, I quote, "without a humane bone in his body" feel under an obligation to help anyone? If such a man as you appear to think I am offers you somewhere to live, it's bound to be to my own advantage, isn't it?' An eyebrow lifted ironically.

Carla's head went back, her eyes closed. It was as though the hammering by the riverside was really in her head.

'You've had enough fresh air for today,' Blaze said sharply. 'I don't want you having a relapse.'

Her too-sweet smile curled her lips and her eyes stayed shut. 'If I died on you, you'd have no one to blame for Crispin's death, would you, Mr Douglas?'

'Don't be sarcastic with me.' Carla's eyes came open at his curtness. He bent down with the intention, it seemed, of lifting her, but her limbs had stiffened in anticipation. His lips, near to hers now, thinned as he said, 'You'd rather I called Rolf from his work to carry you in?'

In a movement which was intended to act as an apology, but which unaccountably turned into a gesture with a deeper meaning, she curled her arm round his neck. A veil was torn down between them and she found herself gazing at the ridge formed by his jaw, the dark shading round his chin telling of a hasty morning shave, catching the scent of the lotion that had been swiftly applied.

Then his mouth caught her attention—they were in the ballroom now—and she saw in close-up the grooves which spread downwards from the full lips.

He stopped and glanced at her, his grey eyes darkening as a thought occurred. He lowered her feet to the floor, keeping one arm round her shoulders. His other hand spread out against the small of her back and she felt herself being urged towards him.

His mouth came to rest on her startled lips. At first his touch was light, then it hardened with an imperative demand. Surprise had widened her eyes; a sweet rush of pleasure closed them. Her hands gripped his shoulders, then one of them moved, waywardly finding his shirt collar and creeping across to find the sharpness of his shoulder-blade.

There was no voice inside her telling her to rebel against his audacity in making her mouth his own. Instead, her every instinct urged compliance. And who am I, she thought dreamily, to tell my intuitive responses that they're wrong?

There was the sound of music and it seemed to be all around them. Voices faded in, laughter and the clink of glasses. *I'm not going to marry you, Crispin . . . Don't be silly, of course you are . . . I'm not . . . Then I'm going to get drunk and you're getting drunk with me . . .*

The party she had attended over three years ago, here in this room—ghostly now, yet still the music played, the voices laughed, laughed almost until they cried . . .

Why had the past returned to haunt her? Did it mean that her subconscious mind was agreeing with Blaze's accusation that she had been guilty of causing the accident? She had, with youthful impetuosity, broken the engagement. Did that mean she would be haunted for the rest of her life by that guilt of which Blaze had accused her?

All the time of her mental struggle, Blaze's lips had been growing more possessive. Now she discovered that her fingers were clutching at his shoulders, that her body was pressed against his and that she was not emitting even the weakest signal that the time had come to end his passionately searching demands. Yet, against her own wish, her limbs tautened, telling her that this man was no Crispin whom she had accepted, then discarded, like an old greetings card. This was an infinitely more dangerous man.

The moment she began to pull away, his head lifted. He noted her white face and frightened eyes. There was a different kind of music now; crashing cymbals and rumbling drums filled her ears. Then Blaze put her from him roughly.

'Is that what my kisses do to you,' he asked scathingly, 'make you afraid? Admit the truth—those large eyes of yours were watching me, willing me to do what I did.'

Carla put a hand to her head. 'No, no, it was the party,' she whispered, 'I heard it, I felt it around me. And Crispin's voice—he was laughing with the others, I swear he was!'

Blaze's hands rested on his narrow hips. His tie had been removed, his shirt was open at the neck. As he listened, his jaw moved as though a decision had been made.

Carla's hands hid her face. 'Maybe you were right. Maybe I should feel guilty.' Her eyes, as she lifted them to his, grew enormous, and as haunted as her ears had been.

A shudder went through her and he caught her under the armpits as the weakness in her legs threatened to make her crumple. He held her against him and she caught at his arms, feeling the hardness of his muscles under her trembling fingers.

He shook her until their eyes entangled. 'You want to exorcise the past?' he asked harshly. His gaze was hypnotic and she was caught in its blinding light. 'There's only one way. Marry me. Become my wife.'

Carla struggled, managing to free herself. All her instincts clamoured, Say yes. This is the man you've remembered since that terrible day. It's been his face that's stayed with you over the passing years, not his brother's, the man you were engaged to. This is the man you truly love . . .

This time her reason argued with her instincts, and her reason won. 'Thank you for the kind offer,' she returned stiffly, 'but the answer's "no". And as for ridding my mind of the past, I don't need help with that. Until I came here, until these last few minutes, it hasn't troubled me at all.'

Those flint-grey eyes had slitted. 'It would be difficult to be more callous than that. You cause your fiancé to die, then you proceed to forget him as if he never existed.'

'That's not true,' she declared. 'Anyway, I'd rather be "haunted" all my life than take such a drastic step as tying myself to you. That would be like inflicting perpetual torment on myself!'

A stride took him against her, a hand gripped her shoulder, the other grasped a handful of hair and dragged back her head. 'Acid-tongued little bitch! Don't goad me too far. I could pick you up, take you down to that boat Rolf Horner's working on and throw you in it, telling you to get the hell out of my life and never come back.'

She had to cling to something to help her stand the pain his hold on her hair was inflicting. Her nails dug into his upper arms. 'You do that, Mr Douglas. I wouldn't go under—I'd survive.' Her eyes defied him. 'I'm a survivor, didn't you know?'

'Oh yes, I know,' he grated, his eyes glacial. '*You* got out of that accident alive. But you made damned sure Crispin didn't!'

Fury overcame her weakness. She swung round, intending to make for the lawn running down to the river, but she did not even make it to the glass doors. Her knees gave way and she sank helplessly to the floor of the large, echoing ballroom.

Blaze came to stand over her crumpled form, but she turned away from the sight of his long, strong legs. His arms lifted her and she had no energy to resist. Her head flopped against him, her cheek finding a strange comfort in the rough hardness of his chest.

With a gentleness that bewildered her—she had not realised that brutality and tenderness could ever go hand in hand within so masculine a body—he took her upstairs to her bedroom and placed her on the bed. 'I'll call Ellen,' he said, and left her alone.

Ellen came in a few minutes later. By then the colour had struggled back to Carla's cheeks.

Ellen smiled. 'I don't know what Mr Douglas was making all that fuss about,' she remarked, twitching the curtains so that they partly covered the windows, making the room darker. 'A little rest is all you need, Miss Howard. First time up after being ill can be exhausting.'

Especially, Carla thought with mirthless amusement, when a quarrel with one's host is thrown in as an optional extra. She lifted her head from the pillow. 'As soon as I've recovered completely, Ellen,' she said, 'I must find somewhere else to live.' Ellen started to protest, but Carla went on, 'I've made up my mind. So,' she managed a smile, 'help me get better quickly, won't you?'

'You know I will, Miss Howard. But you'll have a tussle with Mr Douglas to make him let you leave.'

Carla closed her eyes. 'I've already had a—a fight with him, Ellen. This morning he offered me a permanent home and——'

'You refused?' Carla nodded. 'Ah, I thought he looked angry about something. And he was angry, Miss Howard. Never mind, he'll talk you round.

He's very persuasive when he likes, is Mr Douglas.'

She put a rug over her and Carla thanked her drowsily. It was lunchtime when she awoke. Ellen was at the door again, holding a tray piled with food.

'You're being very good to me,' Carla told her.

'You asked me help you get better quickly, and eating plenty of good food is the best way of doing it.'

'I'll never eat it all, Ellen! Oh, and—Ellen,' she stopped at the door, 'this evening, could I eat downstairs?'

'Of course you can. Mr Douglas will be eating out. Miss Janetta's staying with her brother for a few days.'

Carla pushed away the rug and looked down at herself. 'These are her clothes, Ellen. Should I take them off?'

The housekeeper laughed. 'If you did, what would you wear instead? My clothes?'

Carla smiled at the thought, then sobered. 'Somehow I've got to get myself something to wear.'

'As soon as you're fit, dear, my Herbert will take you shopping in the town. Mr Douglas won't mind him taking one of the smaller cars.'

'Tomorrow, Ellen, could it be tomorrow?'

'Herbert will ask Mr Douglas, and we'll see what he says.'

When Ellen had gone, Carla realised something was missing. She counted on her fingers—clothes, she would be taken shopping to buy them. *To buy* ... For that, a person needed money, and money was something she did not have. There was only one source of cash in that house—its owner. Her heart sank. How could she go cap in hand to Blaze Douglas? After refusing his proposal of marriage, as if it had been a prison cell he'd been offering her with himself as the gaoler, she could not ask him for money now—could she?

Although Carla sat alone at the dining-table, she found it like a tonic to her system to be eating in such surroundings.

The furniture was modern, the dishes equally so in design and colour. Spotlights in the ceiling picked out the two modern wall paintings, the polished pine of the table itself, the smaller table from which the food was served.

She was spooning the soup into her mouth when there were footsteps, followed by a door opening. Since Ellen had just gone, Carla looked up wonderingly.

Blaze appeared through a door in the living area which led directly off the dining-room. He stood in the wide, square archway. 'Play-acting the lady of the house? If you'd accepted my offer of marriage,' his voice mocked, 'you would need more practice in the job. From here, you look like a little girl lost.'

Putting down her spoon, she retorted, 'Then you should be glad I turned you down, shouldn't you? Imagine having to train the woman you married to become the perfect wife!'

He went towards her. 'The only "perfection" I would require would not be in the vicinity of the dining-room.'

To Carla's annoyance, she coloured slightly. 'You'd be disappointed there, too.'

'Really?' Blaze smiled, slipping his hands into the

pockets of his perfectly tailored evening jacket. 'Explain that, will you?'

Fight sparkled in her tilted glance. 'Only if you *explain* your private life first.'

'It would take till dawn. I can think of a better occupation than *talking* all night.'

The jerk of her clasped hands revealed her annoyance. It seems, Carla judged, contemplating his immaculate clothes, that he thinks enough of Janetta Horner to dine *her* expensively. The intimate follow-up to his down-payment in advance of a sumptuous meal probably made it worth his while.

Ellen's voice called, 'Mr Douglas, Miss Janetta's here. Shall I show her in?'

'I'm on my way, Ellen.' He moved away slowly, throwing a sarcastic smile over his shoulder. 'Enjoy your evening. I fully intend to enjoy mine.'

The soup jerked uneasily down Carla's throat. 'I shall appreciate it all the more for your absence from the house.'

If she had expected annoyance, she was disappointed. He replied softly, 'Then I shall have to go away more often, won't I?' His long, firm strides took him on his way.

From the distance came the sound of a high-pitched, welcoming female voice. A car's engine raced, died down and drew away. Likewise, Carla's heartbeats slowed, her adrenalin settled. The whole house felt the emptier for his departure.

The meal over, she wandered through the archway to sink on to the couch. There were ceiling spotlights here, too, illuminating a piece of modern sculpture placed on a stone pedestal; revealing the grain of the polished wood of which the drinks cabinet was made.

The past was not here, only the present. Crispin
had never shown her this part of the house. Maybe
he had been forbidden by his despotic brother to
take his young friends there. And that certainly
included his 'stupid', 'shallow' fiancée. Carla's head
went back, her eyes looked unseeingly at the palely-
lighted ceiling.

Even then, three years ago, Blaze Douglas had
exerted an influence on her life. He disapproved of
her, even refusing to meet her. Then, on that terrible
night, he had blamed her for what had happened.
All those years he had held her in contempt, thought
of her only with anger for, as he thought, curtailing
his brother's life.

Yet here she was, seated in the centre of his luxur-
ious sitting-room, a guest in his house—and the re-
ceiver of his offer of marriage. I was right to refuse,
she told herself defiantly. How could he ever have
thought I'd accept? Yet Blaze Douglas was nobody's
fool. So why had he asked her? And, loving him as
she now knew she did, why, oh, why had she
refused?

CHAPTER FOUR

No sooner had the wheels of Blaze's car stirred the
dust in the parking area at the rear of the house
than another came to catch the dust's descent.

It was Rolf who, a few minutes later, let himself
into the room.

'Hi there, Carla,' he greeted her. 'You've got yourself a visitor.'

Carla smiled, pleased to have company. Without uncurling her legs from under her, she smiled up at Rolf. 'I can't ask you to make yourself at home, because it's not my——'

'That's okay.' He sat in a revolving armchair. 'I've been here so many times it's home from home to me.'

'Is the house along there your real home, Rolf?'

'You sound wistful. Yes, it's mine, but I'm away a lot.'

Her eyes grew dreamy. 'It must be heaven living by the river. If there's nothing else moving on it, the water itself is moving, always changing.'

Rolf nodded. 'Blue with blue skies, grey with grey.' He lifted a shoulder. 'Poetic, aren't we?'

'Don't you care? Doesn't it reach you?' Another shrug greeted her question. 'To me, its movement is like a flow of music.'

'Soft sighing symphonies on tape.'

His cynicism irritated. 'Are you really as materialistic as you make out?' she charged.

'Fast cars, beautiful boats and glamorous women. That's my fantasy world.'

'Janetta too?'

'Fast cars and handsome men. They're my sister's necessities of life.'

'At the moment she's got them both?'

'In Blaze, yes. My sister wouldn't settle for less. I think she's out to land this particular fish. For keeps.'

'Marriage, children, happy ever after?'

'I don't know about the kids. She's restless,

wouldn't like to be tied down by tiny clutching fingers.'

'Does Blaze know her intentions?'

'He'd be pretty dumb if he didn't, and he's not dumb.' Rolf frowned. 'Why so interested in Blaze, Carla?'

Her colour rose. She hoped her dismissing shrug was convincing. She could hardly say, 'This morning he asked me to marry him.' 'He's my host.'

'And?' Rolf swung a little in the chair, his sharp eyes watchful.

Carla uncurled her legs and sat up. 'Don't you know I was engaged to his brother?'

'I know all about Crispin. He was my best friend. All the same, he never said much about you.' His charming smile added a new dimension to his tanned, rounded face. He sat forward, his well-covered body revealing a passion for eating good food. 'Your engagement to his late brother—does that explain your interest in Blaze? There's nothing else?'

Carla affected a frown. 'Should there be?' He surely hadn't heard about Blaze's marriage proposal?

His reply reassured her. 'I sell the new technology, and they say I'm good at my job. Can I sell you myself, Carla?'

So the winding path of their discussion had moved into a clearing. She could see now where it had been leading. 'Go out with you, you mean?'

'For a start. Then——?'

'No "then", Rolf. That's not my game.'

'But Crispin said——'

'Crispin probably said a lot of things about me. I

expect it made his ego feel good.'

'You were good in bed, he said.'

'Thanks for being so blunt, Rolf.' Her eyes grew dull. No wonder Blaze's opinion of her was so low! 'Who am I to dispute the statements of those who are no longer with us?'

Rolf stared at her, then studied his hands. 'Sorry about tripping over *your* ego. I'm sure it wasn't for want of asking on his part.' There was a pause. 'The offer still holds. Would you come out with me? Soon—tomorrow?' He saw her hesitation, and asked, 'Want the hard sell or the soft sell? I'm good at both.' She laughed, which seemed to please him.

'We—ell.' She pretended to consider. 'You're being very obliging by hammering my boat back into shape.'

'Good. I've put you under an obligation, which means you'll come.'

Carla nodded and relaxed against the couch back. The door opened. 'I've made coffee for two, Miss Howard. I know all about Mr Rolf's liking for a cup or two——'

'You timed your entrance very nicely, Ellen,' said Rolf, rising to help wheel in the trolley. He stared at the contents. 'Ellen, you're not to ruin my waist-line!'

'I know your weaknesses, Mr Rolf. All of them.'

Carla looked round at the curious sound in Ellen's voice and found the housekeeper's eyes on her. 'Don't tire yourself, Miss Howard, will you? You've packed a lot into your first day up. No late night, now.'

Rolf laughed. 'My intentions are strictly honourable, Ellen.' As the housekeeper nodded, smiled and went out, Rolf said under his breath, 'For tonight, anyway.'

Carla made no comment. She leant forward to pour the coffee, but Rolf forestalled her. 'Take a rest. I'll do it.' He poured, handed Carla a cup and sat beside her. It was, Carla perceived, a strategic move. Did he hope he might change her mind about the 'and—' before Blaze returned?

As they ate and drank, they chatted about boats. Carla, on her second and last biscuit, sat back and wondered at the amount Rolf was eating. There was, she noticed as she watched him, an enthusiasm about his actions which, despite his twenty-six or so years— the age Crispin would have been had he survived the accident—gave him a childlike air which sat a little uneasily on his mature shoulders.

Rolf wheeled the trolley, minus much of its food, into the hall, calling to Ellen. He returned to his place beside Carla, sitting back, stretching his legs and patting himself. 'Eaten too much,' was his comment.

'That mound will turn into a mountain one day,' Carla observed, smiling.

'Worried about my wellbeing? That's good.' His whole demeanour changed. His arm pushed under her resting head. 'I'll be going soon, so come on, a goodnight kiss. Just one, darling.'

Carla stiffened. He had no right to use the endearment, yet she allowed him to lift her head. At once she regretted her concession. It was all the encouragement he needed. His mouth was on hers, his other arm round her back.

At first she tried to escape, but decided to endure the kiss. It repelled her, but she guessed it would not last. Its length was even shorter than she had anticipated. The door was opened, there was a feminine shriek, followed by high-pitched laughter.

The woman who entered was sophisticated to her fingertips. Her hand rested on Blaze's arm in a manner which told of a knowledge of every sinew and muscle that arm possessed. Her supreme confidence aroused in Carla an immediate resentment. I have everything she has, she told herself, and more— survivability in an unimaginable situation, to start with.

The woman's make-up was perfect, even after dining and dancing. Her fair hair, parted centrally, hung in a silken curtain to her shoulders. The coffee-coloured lacy gown she wore wrapped itself around her slimness, the neckline low-cut enough to delight any male companion. Her present escort, Carla thought sourly, appeared to appreciate everything the lady had to offer.

Rolf stood up at last, glaring at the newcomers.

'Getting to know Blaze's piece of river flotasm, Rolf?' the young woman asked. 'You're making progress, don't you think so, Blaze? My brother never was one to let water flow under bridges before he'd had a chance to dredge the dregs from it.'

Rolf smoothed his hair. 'Apologies, Carla, for my sister's atrocious manners.' He turned to Janetta. 'Since when did I make obnoxious comments on your big love scenes? Keep your sweet little sisterly mouth shut in future, will you?'

Carla ran her hand over the velvet smoothness of the borrowed slacks she was wearing. If she raised her eyes, she knew she would meet Blaze's ice-cold gaze. She was aware that his eyes had not shifted from her from the moment he had entered.

'Has your bait bitten yet, Rolf?' Janetta persisted, determined for some reason to persist with her acid comments. 'Or has she been frightened away by your pressuring methods?'

Rolf replied to his sister indirectly. 'Thanks, Blaze,' he said, 'for keeping my sister out of the way for the evening. She's never objected to my female companions in the past, yet she seems to have taken a particular dislike to Carla.'

Carla's brown eyes lifted unflinchingly to Janetta's. 'Maybe Miss Horner objects to my wearing her clothes?'

'You are?' Janetta looked Carla over. 'I didn't notice. Possibly because I wear them with so much more elegance than you.'

'These are quality clothes, Miss Horner,' Carla flashed back. 'It would be difficult to look anything but elegant in the cut and style of these garments.'

Janetta swung to Blaze. 'I refuse to stand here and be insulted! Take me home, darling. As for those things Miss Howard is wearing, she can keep them. I wouldn't have them back if you paid me.'

Blaze spoke at last. 'Rolf, have you completed your passionate goodnight to Carla?' Carla stared at him, but he went on, 'If so, would you mind taking Janetta home?'

Janetta's arms wound round Blaze's neck. 'What about *our* passionate goodnight, darling?' Her pursed lips urged towards him. His kiss was fleeting, yet told of a familiarity with the owner of the lips which hit Carla like a blow beneath her ribs.

Automatically she smiled as Rolf, at the door, lifted a hand, saying, 'Tomorrow afternoon, three o'clock?'

Carla cursed herself for her quick glance at Blaze. Why had her first thought been to seek his permission? His eyes slewed round to her, narrowed and cold. So he objected, did he?

'Tomorrow at three,' she answered with spirit, watching Blaze as he showed them from the room.

Carla relaxed against the cushions. It had been a long day, but something told her it was not over yet. From the rear of the house came the sound of a car driving away. Only a few moments now until Blaze was back . . . Carla discovered that her palms were moist.

Voices came from the kitchen area and a discussion seemed to be taking place. It ended and Blaze came in, walking over to her.

'Herbert has just asked permission to borrow one of my smaller cars to take you shopping tomorrow.'

Carla nodded. 'Ellen told me he would. Is it all right?'

'I told him I had no objection. But haven't you forgotten something?'

Carla frowned, then her brow cleared. 'Oh, you mean money.' It was a problem which could be solved by only one thing. 'I—I have a small sum in savings which I haven't touched——'

'Do you mean this?' He took something from his pocket. With an assessing look he noted her whitening cheeks. 'Ellen found it in your purse which we recovered from the boat. It was tucked well away. You kept this ring, you told me, for the day you reached rock-bottom.'

Her throat felt dry, but her hand reached out. 'Will you give it to me, please?'

He bounced the ring on his palm. 'Why, have you reached that state? Do you now need to sell it?'

'It's no business of yours whether I do or not.' He went on tossing the ring. Carla struggled to her feet, ignoring the weakness that washed over her. She had known this particular day would prove endless. Would she never get to bed? 'Please give me that ring,' she repeated, determinedly hiding her mounting desperation.

Blaze held in his hand her talisman, her protection from destitution, her only means of obtaining money in any quantity. He laughed derisively as he watched her clenched hands press her knuckles white. All the while he continued to play idly with the ring which, as he was well aware, represented her freedom from dependence on others, and most of all, himself.

Her eyes followed the diamond and ruby ring as it jumped up and down, up and down. Something snapped and she was confronting him, grasping his arm and clawing at his closed hand. 'Give it to me!' she cried. 'It's mine—Crispin gave it to me. I need it, I have to have it——'

He freed himself with a single movement. 'Why?' he snarled. 'To buy yourself back into respectability?' He threw the ring across the room and she was after it, scratching in the carpet pile to find it. Feet strode from behind her and she was lifted from her crouching position. Hands under her arms gripped and held her up, turning her. 'Marry me,' Blaze commanded, 'my name will give you all the respectability you want.'

'You can keep your name!' she shrieked. 'I don't want it and I don't want you. All I want is the means to live decently, eat adequately, earn a reasonable wage. As for respectability, I've never lost it. As long as a person's mind stays good and honest, what do outside appearances matter?'

'Why did you agree to marry my brother if not for his money and social position, and what is all that if not "respectability"? You took my brother's ring and when you'd ended his life, you kept the ring. It represented money, didn't it? You admitted that yourself. So when has *your* mind been "good and honest"?'

Her hand found her head and she sank into the nearest chair. She found that her hand was shaking. Recovering her composure, she lifted her head proudly. 'All through those weeks without proper shelter, with no place to call my own, no income, nothing, I never once lost my honesty, nor my dignity.'

Blaze Douglas stood, hands on hips, shirt sleeves rolled, his breathing deep and steady. He regarded her inscrutably.

Something caught Carla's eye. A diamond glinted, a ruby stained with red the white tufts of a rug. Slowly she rose, reached out to pick up the ring and turning, held it out. Blaze looked at it, at the shaking hand that was offering it to him, then he took it and slipped it into his pocket.

Quietly, Carla said, 'Thank you for your offer of marriage, but I refuse it totally. I'll stay here until my health is back to normal. After I've gone, I'll save somehow and eventually pay you for every bit of hospitality you've offered me.'

Leaving him, she went to the door, opened it and, without turning, went up to bed.

*

Carla rose early next morning. Pulling back the curtains, she felt the warmth of the sun penetrating the glass of the windows. Velvet slacks would not suit such a day.

Reluctantly, she looked through Janetta's clothes. Since her only source of ready cash had gone from her, there was no alternative. Even if Blaze gave her back the ring, she decided defiantly, she wouldn't take it, not after the terrible things he had accused her of last night.

The clothes all had a similarity of quality and boldness of design which went neither with her own personality nor her usual choice of style. The name 'Janetta' might have been sewn into the label with that of the designer. Sighing, she went on searching.

The dress she finally chose was sleeveless and had a deceptively simple cut, with rounded neckline and belted waist. It was the design of the fabric which conflicted with her preference for simplicity. Over the background colour of pale blue were wide, diagonal blocks of black, stretching from neck to hem.

One glance in the mirror was sufficient to bring her teeth snapping shut. The dress probably looked devastating on its true owner. On her, despite its famous label, it looked cheap.

Going down to breakfast, she crossed her fingers that Blaze would be anywhere but at the table. To her dismay, she found him watching her wandering in the entrance hall, studying doors and wondering which to open.

'Looking for something?' he asked, his eyes all over the boldly-patterned dress.

'I—wasn't sure where breakfast was served. In the dining-room, or——?'

'Are you trying to make me believe you really don't know the layout of this house?'

'I really don't know it. I only know that—that big room——' she pointed.

'And Crispin's bedroom? Or are you going to tell me again that you've never been in that room before this past week or so? From what Crispin used to tell me——'

Her shoulders lifted. 'All right, you've got me fixed in your mind as Crispin's woman, and nothing I say will change your mind. Please,' her tone altered, her brown eyes grew appealing, 'will you tell me where I can eat? I'm empty right here,' she pressed herself, 'and my digestive juices are crying out for work to do.'

He laughed for the first time and Carla's heart did a somersault. His face came alive. It was like a burst of sunshine lighting up a snow-capped mountain peak and melting the snow instantly. For a few precious seconds he became approachable and Carla's heart hammered as if she had already started scaling the heights . . .

'It's a good sign,' Blaze remarked. 'Shows you must be almost back to normal. This way.' He opened a door.

'So it won't be long now before you get me off your back—and your mind,' she rejoined, looking round the small, simply-furnished room where breakfast awaited them.

'Mm, throw you back in the river, you mean? Watch you floundering and begging for me to rescue you.' He pretended to consider, eyes still on the dress—or the shape beneath it. Carla could not decide. 'The idea's pleasing, very pleasing indeed.'

'It's nice to know I'm so welcome in your house,' she responded tartly. 'Don't worry, I'll find somewhere else soon—even if it means sleeping on my friend's floor.'

Ellen appeared round the half-open door. 'How many eggs with your bacon, Miss Howard, one or two? Only one? You'll never get fit if you don't eat properly.'

Carla took her seat and Blaze sat to her right at the oval-shaped table. 'I'm fit now, really I am,' she called after Ellen. 'I never did have a large appetite.'

'It shows,' Blaze commented critically. 'You're too thin.'

'For whose taste? If it's yours, it doesn't matter, does it, since I've said "no, thank you" to your proposal of marriage.'

Blaze considered for a moment, then returned calmly, 'If I took "no" for an answer as many times as it's been said to me in the course of my business life, I wouldn't have the thriving company of Douglas Business and Information Equipment under my control.'

Carla's eyes fired to life. 'If I were ever stupid enough to marry you, Mr Douglas,' she queried over-sweetly, 'would I become just another part of your "business equipment"?'

His eyes flickered narrowly in response. 'If you married me, Miss Howard, you would become part of *me*.'

Herbert drove Carla to the best department store in town, waited at the kerb until she entered through the swing doors, then drove to find a parking place.

Aimlessly at first, Carla wandered from the cosmetics section, through jewellery to handbags and evening purses. The store was known to her. She was doing now what she had often done in the past—pausing to admire, sigh and pass on. Except that this time she was not sighing.

There was no intention in her mind of purchasing a single thing. Without money, cheque book or credit card, she could do nothing. They had all been in the boat and must, she was sure, have sunk to the river bed when the boat had tipped almost on to its side.

Her feet took her of their own accord upstairs to ladies' clothing. It was a store whose prices were beyond her pocket, yet which drew her always like a magnet. Her taste was good even though her supply of money was not. A woman assistant looked at her, her attention caught by the dress Carla wore.

The assistant approached. 'Please excuse my curiosity, madam, but isn't that one of our dresses? Do you know,' she ignored Carla's slightly bewildered shake of the head, 'I can remember seeing an order on behalf of a special customer . . . Never mind, even if I can't remember her name,' she turned and led Carla towards a rack of dresses, 'I'm sure I can interest you in a few very suitable items.'

'It's kind of you, but——'

'It will be a pleasure, madam. And a challenge, if I may say so, finding colours to complement your beautiful hair. Now this long-sleeved dress——'

'I wasn't intending to buy,' Carla interrupted, anxious now. How could she tell a sales assistant she had no money?

'Oh, but you can open an account with us, madam. Quite simple——' She slipped the dress from the hanger. 'Of course—you're Miss Howard,' her ingenuous smile was surely contrived, Carla hazarded, 'all your purchases are to be placed on your fiancé's account. This way to the changing rooms, Miss Howard. Yes, Mr Douglas phoned, instructing us to give you all the help we can in filling your wardrobe with all the kind of clothes you'll need as his wife.'

'But I'm not——'

'Now, while you're trying that dress on, I'll look out some other items—evening gowns, don't you think? Do slacks suits appeal to you? Leisure outfits, of course.' She was gone.

Carla sank helplessly on to the chair, clasping her bag. Seeing her despondency reflected back by the mirror, she counted to three and came to a decision. Straightening her back, she resolved that she wouldn't even try to resist the woman's expert salesmanship. She would accept whatever was suggested, leave them to be delivered, then, just before Rolf came to collect her that afternoon, she would call the store and cancel the entire order.

She had reckoned, however, without the sales lady's persistence and expertise. Even as Carla had selected the garments, they had been packed.

'The whole amount,' the assistant murmured, 'will, as directed, be put on Mr Douglas's account. No trouble, madam, no trouble at all. And may I wish you every happiness in your married life?'

Herbert, having stood at a discreet distance, escorted her to the car. The back seat of the vehicle had been piled high with boxes. The tall wooden doors leading to the rear of the house had been opened and Herbert drove on, braking in front of the main entrance.

Carla thrust open the car door, thanked Herbert over her shoulder and hurried up the steps. It was Blaze she was after. She came to an abrupt stop as she realised she did not know where he was.

Ellen emerged. 'Mr Douglas? In his office, dear. Did you find some nice dresses?'

'A lot of things, Ellen. Please—where's the office?'

'That door, Miss Howard,' Herbert indicated with a nod, coming into the house laden with boxes. At once Ellen took charge, preceding him up the stairs. It was the chance Carla had been waiting for.

With a brief knock she burst into Blaze's office. It was a large room, and daylight streamed in through windows which were thrown open. The desk was littered with folders, piles of paper, scattered sheets bearing diagrams. Everywhere there were pictures, posters of alien shapes, screens and cabinets. The chairs and desks in the photographs were out of this world, too. Looking at them made Carla feel like an Alice in a very strange Wonderland. Her gaze and her mind came homing back. 'This is your business— marketing these?' She found Blaze's sardonic eyes upon her. He nodded.

'Impressed?'

'How can I be,' she returned, 'when I might as well be in a space capsule for all the meaning these pieces of machinery have for me?'

Blaze handed her some leaflets. 'Work-stations,' she read 'lateral and rotational adjustments', 'con- soles' and 'ergonomic features'. With a shake of her head, she placed the leaflets beside him. 'I'm no wiser, but thanks.'

He nodded, then asked blandly, 'Didn't Ellen tell

you I tolerate no interruptions while I'm at my desk?'

'Didn't *I* tell you that, first—I didn't want your money and second, *I am not going to marry you?*' His reflective smile, at the paper on which he was writing, was like a thorn on a rose bush drawing her blood. 'You set the trap for this morning, didn't you?' she stormed.

'And didn't you fall into it nicely!' he responded with deep amusement. 'Herbert phoned me when he'd parked the car. You went straight into the shop without a murmur of protest, he said. A bit of psychological reasoning told me that, being a woman, you'd make eventually for the women's department. I'd even telephoned the chief saleswoman there and described the dress you were wearing.'

'Janetta's dress!'

His eyes were on his work again. 'There was nothing I could do about that.'

'Well, you may like to know that I'm having every single item returned to the store.'

Blaze threw down his pen and rose slowly. Hands in pockets, he confronted her. Without warning, his hands were gripping her arms so cruelly she cried out. 'If you return those clothes,' he snarled, 'I'll have them sent back here. If you still don't see sense, I promise you I shall lock you in your room until you do. Am I making myself clear?'

'Who do you think you are?' she raged. 'You are *not* my fiancé. I *refuse* to marry you. Nothing you can do will make me.'

'Oh no?' he countered, pulling her against him. In vain she attempted to shake free of him, only to find his hold softening, his arms slipping round her.

His change of tactics took her by surprise. He had broken through her defences not with a bulldozer but with the finesse of an accomplished horserider leaping over a fence. Irritation gave strength to her hands which pushed at his shoulders. His mouth touching hers, catching her parted, protesting lips, turned that strength into weakness.

Her arms slid to his shoulders, one of them curving round his neck. Her mouth was being plundered and her senses reeled. When the zip fastener at the back of the dress came sliding down she was in no state to tell him 'no'. The skin of her back tingled under his skimming hands and she felt herself straining to hold him, giving kiss for searching kiss.

After his head had lifted, without letting her go, he smiled faintly into her love-drugged eyes. It was the smile of conquest, of the achievement of a goal, and it maddened her. Her twisting and turning freed her at last. She reached round to her back and re-fastened the zip. 'I'm still going to send those clothes back to the store.' While speaking, she had prepared herself for flight. She had almost reached the door when he caught her, swinging her round and scooping her into his arms. It was no gesture of warmth, nor of play, this she could see by the set of his mouth.

'I gave you warning, but you've chosen to ignore it. Now you'll take the consequences.'

'No, no, Blaze! I've got a date with Rolf this afternoon.'

'Rolf Horner can go hang himself—from a mast, if he likes.'

They were halfway up the stairs now. 'If you lock me in, I'll call for Ellen. She'll let me out——'

'At the cost of her job. And her husband's.'

They were in her room now and he set her on her feet. 'You wouldn't,' she gasped, wide-eyed, 'you wouldn't dismiss them just like that!'

The hardness in his eyes was sufficient confirmation of his statement.

'Then you're the most unscrupulous, pitiless man I know!'

At the door, he said, 'You'd do well to remember that.'

'Blaze,' she clasped her hands, 'you're not going to leave me like this? Shut in here . . .'

'I have every intention of shutting you in here until you come to your senses.'

'I've—I've come to them, Blaze. I'll keep the clothes.'

He walked menacingly towards her and Carla forced herself not to back away. 'Do you know something—I don't trust you.' He glanced around. 'Crispin's room. I hope his memory, plus those you made while you both occupied his bed, return to haunt you in your solitude.' He went out, returned and said, 'Your food will be brought to you by Ellen. She will attend to all your needs.'

'Blaze,' Carla tried a final plea, 'what would change your mind and let you free me?'

His narrowed gaze scrutinised her in detail and she pushed her wayward hair from flushing cheeks.

'You're appealing for a truce? Good. I'll make the terms hard—your willing agreement to our marriage.'

'I'll never give that,' she declared in a whisper.

'Then we'll just have to do without the legalities, won't we? No ring—and *no vows*.'

CHAPTER FIVE

ELLEN made sure that Carla had her meals, washed whenever she wanted, and was given magazines and books.

'All I want, Ellen,' Carla said tearfully, after her evening meal, 'is my liberty. I'd go hungry and cold if it meant being free again. I've done it before. *Please*, Ellen?'

'It's more than my job's worth, Miss Howard, to leave that door unlocked.'

'Just suppose, Ellen——' Carla's deeply brown eyes crinkled slightly at the corners, 'just suppose, in the night, I needed——'

Ellen smiled back, and went out, saying nothing.

Carla went to bed early and tossed and turned. Her skin as well as her emotions had grown overheated and she threw off the covers. When she heard the sound of a key turning, her breathing stopped, hoarding itself for the scream which tautened her vocal chords.

The scream was never uttered. When her breathing resumed, it turned into a gasp. Blaze was in the room, inserting the key and relocking the door. Deprived of speech, Carla watched his dark shape as he wandered to the bed, hands in the pockets of his black robe. He reached for the bedside lamp and switched it on.

'What do you want?' Carla asked, so alarmed she just lay and stared.

'You.'

'I've—I've said "no" to your proposal. How many times have I——?'

' "No" is a negative reaction. When I'm doing a deal, I believe in the positive approach.'

'This isn't a business deal.' Her mouth was dry with fright, her brown eyes large in the lamp's glow.

'It isn't?' he drawled. 'Then I take you as I said— no ring, no vows?' He loosened his robe, letting it drop to the ground. His uncovered body gleamed broadly and, to her fascinated eyes, held immense power. Hands found his hips. His eyes roamed over her reclining form, her head held tautly away from the pillow.

'Maybe you're right,' he said softly. 'More of a coercion by my opponent, with her half-veiled beauty unbalancing my judgment and making me almost forget I'm a gentleman.' His smile was as derisive as his words.

Carla looked down at herself and the pink of her see-through gown—another of Janetta's—invaded her cheeks. She had forgotten her lack of adequate covering! As she reached to tug at the covers she had discarded, Blaze leaned across the large bed and gripped her wrist.

'Leave it.' He stretched out beside her, his grey eyes taunting. 'Now cover us both.'

'I told you,' she choked, 'I'm not going to marry you!'

He turned on to his side, resting on his elbow. 'Who said anything about marriage, my lovely?'

'Oh, no, you're not!' she vowed, and swung her legs to the floor, forgetting that the door was locked. She stood facing it, her hands flat on its surface as if pushing it would make it open. Her head drooped and she was forced to acknowledge that he had won.

When she turned, she found him laughing at her predicament. With little to cover her from his mocking, fascinated gaze, she had no alternative but to return to the bed. If only she could grab his robe from the other side of the bed ...

Anticipating her intention, he swung from the bed and threw the robe at the door even as she sped away from it towards him. 'Oh!' she cried, furious now, and turning back to the door. An arm lifting formed a barrier, even more formidable than the first. His hard, angled body collided with hers, knocking the air from her lungs. All her struggles to escape were frustrated with consummate ease by his lazy strength. At last she conceded defeat, lying back against him, her head against his shoulder.

His arm moved upwards from her waist to cover her breasts, his other arm joined it. Locked together with him, she felt her blood sing in her veins. Slowly, slowly his body began to sway behind her, taking her pliant body with it.

It was as though they were engaged in a timeless sensual dance to the sound of the music filling her mind. They took the rhythm from each other's limbs, moving slowly and in perfect accord as if they were dancing to the same compelling tune.

'Give me your mouth,' he murmured. She obeyed unhesitatingly, her willpower completely under his control. His head bent over her shoulder, meeting her lips and caressing them with his. Her arms lifted to cover those around her and even when his kiss was over, limbs still swayed against limbs, the softness of hers stroking the hardness of his.

When his hold changed and he scooped her up, her head lolled on his chest. She throbbed with desire and when he lowered her to the bed and lay beside her again, she found her entire self wanting him to make her his. Her eyes opened and lingered on every feature of his face. Even as she whispered his name, she acknowledged again that she had fallen completely and irreversibly in love with him.

He touched her with his eyes. 'Tomorrow,' he said, 'we shall marry.'

Mutely she nodded, waiting, waiting for her love for him to open the doors to the feelings he must surely have for her.

'Do you hear me?' His sharpness was like a cold wind dispersing the mists around her mind.

'Yes, yes, Blaze.' Her cheeks were warm, the fire he had lit inside her burned unquenchably.

His tone softened just a little as he said, 'I have a licence and the rings. I bought them a few days ago.'

'You were that sure of me?'

'Of myself. Does that make you hate me?'

Carla shook her head. 'Nothing would make me do that.'

His finger ran down from her neck to rest between her breasts. 'There's hope for our marriage, then.' His smile was fleeting and sardonic. 'Here,' his arm lifted, 'come to me.'

She went, without demur. He crushed her to him and ran a hand lightly over her breasts, her hips and thighs. Then it lifted to stroke back her hair. In a state of torment, she waited—and waited. 'You're the most beautiful woman I've ever seen,' he said softly. 'You won't escape me now. Tomorrow you'll become my wife. Tonight I'm going to make you my lover.'

His lips found the hollow of her neck and she shivered under his caress. His mouth moved and found the curving softness of her, bringing every part to leaping life. Slowly his hard-skinned fingers grazed the smooth softness of her breasts. He lowered the straps of the nightgown, finally easing it right away and dropping it heedlessly to the floor.

Carla's own fingers gripped his shoulders, tightening as his lips tantalised her soft flesh into filling hardness. She gave willingly, rapturously as his desire sought to master and conquer. The music in her mind grew louder, its primitive drumbeat stirring her to an abandonment which she knew instinctively that his male needs demanded.

The time was fast approaching when she would become irrevocably his, and she wanted to whisper, Take care, oh, please take care. The words did not leave her lips, but when the moment came his gentleness was such that with the joy came tears, tears of gratitude for his infinite care.

They lay at last enfolded and at peace, and she knew just how strongly her love for this man had taken root. It was a long time before Blaze stirred. When he did, he propped his head on his hand and smiled down into her wondering eyes.

His lips nuzzled her ear and a thrill of pleasure shot through her as her sensitivity stirred again to anticipatory life.

'How did you know, Blaze?' she asked, her hand pushing back his hair.

'That you'd never been with a man? By your responses. You followed wherever I led, as if you were in a maze and only I held the key to it.' He kissed the tip of her nose. 'I told you, sweetheart, that I'd win. You're my wife now,' he mouthed against her lips, 'and tomorrow, as I said, we'll marry.'

'You said no vows, no legalities. Why,' she asked mischievously, 'did you change your mind?'

'I want to bind you to me, that's why, my river lady.'

'What if I said "no"?' she provoked.

'Then I'd abduct you and take you forcibly to the ceremony.'

A lovely weariness came over her and she sighed from her depths. 'Oh, Blaze, I want to marry you. If I hadn't loved you before, I'd love you now.' Her arm reached out to rest on his chest.

He turned to his side and gathered her to him. 'So you love me. It sounds good to my ears. Did it sound good to Crispin's ears when you said the same words to him?'

Carla was almost asleep. The question had come so softly, so nebulously through the mists of tiredness, she knew she had dreamt it.

A hand was shaking her shoulder, but it was Ellen's hand. Carla discovered she was alone in the bed.

'It's your wedding day, Miss Howard,' Ellen was saying. 'Yes, dear, Mr Douglas told me. Isn't it wonderful you're going to marry into the family after all? First Mr Crispin's fiancée, now Mr Douglas's.'

Carla half sat up, dragging the covers to her chin. 'I still can't believe it, Ellen. When he said yesterday he wouldn't let me out of here until I said "yes", I didn't believe him.'

'I did, Miss Howard. I thought to myself, well, he

really means to get her for himself! When it's something Mr Douglas wants, he never gives up until he's got it, no matter what it is.'

Carla thought, he was determined to 'get' me, although I still don't know why. He's won and now I belong to him . . . She remembered her nightdress. For heaven's sake, she panicked, where is it? Ellen mustn't find it. What would she think? Something soft was touching her leg. Blaze had pushed it into the bed beside her! She sighed with relief at his thoughtfulness.

'I'll be down for breakfast soon, Ellen,' she announced.

'No need, Miss Howard. I've had instructions from Mr Douglas to bring your breakfast up to you. Mr Douglas has gone out. He said to tell you he'd see you at the ceremony just before three o'clock this afternoon. Herbert and I are coming. Wasn't it nice of Mr Douglas to ask us?'

'Do you know if there's going to be a best man, Ellen?'

'Oh, Mr Douglas is doing it all properly. Your brother's going to be best man, Miss Howard. Now isn't that nice?'

'My *brother*? How does he know about it? Did Mr Douglas contact him?' Ellen was nodding vigorously. 'What—what about Rolf, Rolf Horner? And his sister?'

Ellen shook her head. 'Mr Rolf's away on business today, and Miss Janetta wasn't invited.'

This piece of news delighted Carla. Had Blaze guessed that she wouldn't have wanted Janetta Horner at her wedding?

'Did Rolf come for me yesterday afternoon, Ellen?'

she asked.

The housekeeper nodded. 'Mr Douglas sent him off with his tail between his legs, and no nonsense. Mr Douglas said you were going to be his wife and he wouldn't have you going out with anyone else, even if the man was an old friend of the family.'

'He said that yesterday *afternoon*, Ellen?'

'He did, Miss Howard. Mr Rolf was very surprised and went off shaking his head.'

Carla shook her own head. Blaze had been so sure of himself he was spreading the news, hours before she herself knew it, that she was going to marry him?

'When you've had your breakfast, Miss Howard,' said Ellen, 'there's a lady coming from the big store in the town. She's bringing a selection of outfits for you to choose from. Mr Douglas's orders.'

'Oh, but——'

'I looked through those lovely things you bought yesterday, when I unpacked them, Miss Howard, but there's nothing there suitable for you to get married in.'

'I suppose you're right, Ellen. When's she coming?'

'Ten, Miss Howard.'

'I'll be ready.'

Carla was, and when she went down to welcome the woman, she recognised her as being the sales lady who had served her yesterday. In the living area, the outfits were spread over chairs and couches.

Finally, Carla chose a cream silk dress and jacket, buying accessories and sandals to match from the assortment which the sales lady had brought with her.

'I think you've chosen well, Miss Howard,' the woman said. 'It sets off the colour of your beautiful hair, plus the look of—well, fragility about you, if I may say so.'

Carla smiled, thinking, I'm tough, there's nothing breakable about me. Except, a fugitive voice whispered, your heart.

There was a small reception after the ceremony at a restaurant in the town. A handful of Blaze's business colleagues and their wives attended, and Ellen, radiating a motherly kind of happiness, mixed with the guests, trailed wherever she went by Herbert.

Nigel, Carla's brother, seemed a changed man. Carla remembered his unrepentant dismissal of her from his household and thought, a little acidly, it's wonderful what the scent of money in the air can do to a callous relative!

Pauline, his wife, was suitably and yet fashionably dressed, and her manner, likewise, had changed for the better. Even to Blaze, she talked with convincing pleasure of the approach of the birth of Nigel's and her baby. Blaze, however, merely smiled and nodded and lost no time in moving away. Carla, a little sickened by Pauline's slightly obsequious manner, followed him with her eyes and wondered what he felt.

For a few moments she stood alone, wondering if she had sunk lower in his estimation for possessing such a family. It was plain by his still uncommitted attitude even after the passionate night, and even after marrying her, that he did not love her. She lifted the shoulder spray of flowers that adorned her jacket and inhaled their sweet perfume, releasing them with care to lie against her as colourfully as before.

What use to wonder why this, why that? Blaze Douglas was now her husband. She had all the security a woman could want. Materially, she would never again be in need. If, during the rest of her life, her emotions should wither away for want of nourishment, then—

'Sweetheart?' Blaze was beside her, his hands holding her upper arms in an open and credible display of affection. Ellen and Herbert, arm in arm, were as one in their smiling audience participation. Other guests smiled with them. Now I know, Carla thought, not without bitterness, the reason for the endearment.

She gazed up at him, her hair, having been released from the small hat she had worn, springing free and glowing. Her eyes glowed, too, the brown of them shining with a love she truly felt, but which made his lips twitch with irony. 'Yes, darling?' she asked softly.

'My bride standing alone on her wedding day?'

'You deserted me.' She managed a pout.

'Then you should have come after me, demanding your rights.'

Carla's brow pleated in a playful frown. 'What rights should I have demanded, darling?'

There were laughing comments of 'You asked for that, Blaze,' and, 'Haven't you got farther than holding her hand, Blaze?'

Blaze pulled her closer to his side. 'Well,' he looked down at her, 'have I, darling?'

Memories of what had happened in the night

brought a bright colour to her cheeks. 'My memory's so short, Blaze,' she answered provocatively, 'that I can't remember things from one minute to the other.'

Again there was laughter, and the guests drifted away. 'Top of the class for tact, my love,' he remarked satirically. 'You'll do well as a chief executive's wife.'

'Thank you for those kind words, even if they are the height of arrogance,' she flared. 'You found treasure washed up on your mooring platform instead of the scum of the river world, did you?' He had angered and hurt her by his coolly detached assessment of her qualities. Had he already forgotten the precious moments of lovemaking which, in the small hours, had made them as one? It was plain, she thought bitterly, that that 'oneness' had to him been purely physical. Had that been just a kind of paradise island in the stormy sea that was to be their marriage?

'You considered me "too stupid" and "too shallow" to marry your brother,' she heard herself saying. 'Has three years improved me so much that I'm now qualified to take up the highly-prized, excellently rewarded position as your wife?'

'You're spoiling for a fight, are you? Maybe I was too gentle with you last night, after all.' His eyes had turned cold, but only she could see their drop in temperature, since his back was to the guests. He seized her wrist and turned. 'Carla and I are leaving you to it. Thanks for your good wishes—not to mention your gifts.'

They left to shouts of repeated congratulations and glasses held high. Blaze's car stood outside and he saw Carla into it. Ellen came running out, threw a handful of confetti over them both and hurried back, laughing. 'See you both tomorrow, Mr Douglas,' she called, waving.

'Why tomorrow?' Carla asked, brushing herself as Blaze swung the car towards the road.

'I've given Ellen and Herbert the rest of the day off. They're staying overnight with some friends. It was Ellen's suggestion.'

In the entrance hall, they faced each other. Her fighting mood had worked itself out of her system. Her smile was uncertain, his gaze beyond her interpretation. 'I—I must change,' she said.

'You have already,' he deliberately misunderstood, 'devastatingly. Last night you were a pretty young girl, now you're a ravishingly lovely woman.'

She affected a frown. 'Now I wonder who was responsible for that?'

His laughter was deep and with her finger she traced the curve of his mouth.

'We'll go out, take the car, then walk,' he told her. 'Wear something suitable, Carla.'

She nodded and hurried upstairs.

The wardrobe was filled with her own clothes. Janetta's had been packed up and returned to her. Yet the wraith-like image of the other girl persisted. Her clothes might have gone, but the reality of her remained. I might be Blaze's wife, Carla reflected, feeling strangely threatened, but will I ever be his only woman?

Blaze glanced up the stairs as she descended, looking with masculine assessment at the slim shape beneath the beige slacks of the suit she had chosen, and the silky matching blouse which pulled tautly across her breasts. The jacket hung from her finger and was draped over her shoulder.

It was not an outfit she would normally have worn for walking, but how often, she had argued, did a woman celebrate the first day of her marriage? And why shouldn't she carry over the feeling of happiness which still persisted to the remaining hours of this supposedly blissful day?

Arriving a little breathless at the foot of the stairs, she asked him, 'Will I do?'

'Until tonight, you'll do very nicely,' he replied, smiling tormentingly.

Hoping to equal him, she pretended coolness at his meaningful words, but her pulse rate speeded at the dictate of her quivering heart.

They took the route to the countryside which bordered the small town, crossing the elegant suspension bridge, turning left and driving along a road which seemed to head straight for a climbing expanse of woodland. Carla had been there once before, and it was Crispin who had taken her. When they had arrived in that exact spot, however, he had decided that the climb would be too strenuous and turned back.

This man beside her possessed a stouter heart and tougher muscles. Brothers they might have been, but their characters were different in every respect— except in one important way. They both got exactly what they wanted, Crispin in the past and Blaze now. Hadn't Blaze said he consistently refused to accept the answer 'no'? And hadn't he 'won', as he claimed? And wasn't she even now, with the wedding ring still strange on her finger, his wife in fact as well as name? And his lover, too?

CHAPTER SIX

BLAZE looked at Carla, then at the tree-covered hill in front of them. 'There's a road which will take us to the top, or there's a path through those woods. It's quite a climb. Do we drive or do we walk?'

Carla gazed at the rising sea of green in front of them. 'Let's walk.' She flashed him a smile. 'Is that what Janetta would have answered?'

'No,' he drawled, pausing as he opened his door, 'and you damned well know it.'

With a grin, Carla got out, turning her smile on to him again. 'Don't tell me, Janetta would have waited for you to do the gentlemanly thing and come round to open this door for her.'

'You're fishing for the compliment,' he returned, half smiling and looking down at her, his hands on his hips, 'so here it is. You're right. You're very different from Rolf's sister. Does that please you?'

'In what way, Blaze?' He had secured the car and they had started walking.

'Every way. Why else do you think I married you?'

They were climbing and the leaves and branches stretched high to meet the late afternoon sky. Carla frowned. 'I don't know, Blaze, I truly don't know.' The gold band, topped by the diamond and platinum engagment ring he had pushed into place later, seemed suddenly to weigh heavily on her finger.

Their hands met, swinging and touching. Somehow her hand and his were clasped and she turned a radiant face towards him. The climb was steep, as he had said, but it was bringing a brightness to her eyes which reflected into the greyness of his, flecking them with golden brown.

He tugged her to a stop and pulled her to face him. His arms went round her, wrapping her to him, and she felt all his masculine hardness the length and breadth of her. His mouth fitted on to hers, taking her parted lips on a gasp, exploring the moistness he found there and testing the sharpness of her teeth.

It was their first kiss since the marriage ceremony. As the lovemaking the night before had united them on the physical plane, so this meeting of their mouths made them one in a different way. A kiss, she thought dreamily, that seems to speak—but what is Blaze telling me? If only it were of his love, she agonised.

They drew apart and his eyes probed into her very being. Hers searched and searched again for the tenderness of the night before. He found her hand and they walked on beneath the stirring trees, which sang in their own way as the darting, winging birds gave voice to their own particular joys of living.

They trod on a hard path strewn with leaf layers put down by passing years. His strides were longer than hers and she found herself hastening to catch up. His legs were encased in beige slacks that wrapped around his thighs, pulling tautly across his lean hips. His shirt was a dark brown, and the outline of his chest and shoulders stretched the cotton fabric, letting the sharpness of his shoulder blades through. A lightweight zipped jacket hung over his shoulder.

At last they emerged from the woods into the open. They had reached the summit and the view opened out at their feet. There was the familiar patchwork design of the countryside spreading to the horizon. Down in the valley, the River Thames wound its quiet way, while here and there a boat drifted into sight.

Blaze walked ahead and, linked as they were, Carla was made to follow. He found a part of the hill that pleased him and he urged her down to sit on his jacket and at his side. The branches of a tree provided an interlacing of green against the blue, cloud-scattered sky. It was a shelter, too, from others who walked by, ignoring them, their eyes caught by the landscape which spread below.

Blaze took her hand and looked at his rings, then tossed a smug smile at her.

'Go on,' she jeered, 'say it. "I've won."'

He flicked her cheek. 'I've won. I told you, when I'm doing a deal, I don't give up until I clinch it the way I want it.' He pushed her down, then hovered over her, grasping her chin. 'I clinched you last night, didn't I, in more ways than one.'

Carla grabbed at his shirt collar, tugging it. 'Why, you——!'

He gripped her wrists and forced them back against the grass. 'Be honest and say it was what you wanted, too. Tell me the truth, that I made you happy. Tell me you love me.'

Her brown eyes widened, telling him the answer

before she spoke. 'You made me ecstatically happy, Blaze,' she whispered. 'And I love you, I love you——'

'And you'll never run away from me.'

She moistened her lips and echoed, 'I'll never run away from you.'

He released her, taking a handful of her hair each side of her face. 'Pure gold, but more precious.' He put each one to his lips.

'No dross?' she joked. 'River flotsam isn't usually plated with the real thing.'

'Impudent puss!' He moved across her, deftly unfastening the buttons of her top. His hand forced an entrance, taking possession of the curving breast beneath. The pressure of his body compressed his hand against her. Even so, it moved, down to her waist, stroking, persuading until her arms lifted and curled about his back, satisfying the hunger of his lips with an appetite of her own.

'My wife,' he said softly, ending the kiss at last, 'my lovely wife.'

He had lifted away from her, yet still his hand possessed her.

Her hand lifted shakily to push his hair aside. 'We shouldn't lie here like this,' she reproved, smiling. 'In public——'

'We're married. If anyone asks,' he looked around at the nearest group, some distance away, 'I can wave this in front of them.' He reached into his back pocket and withdrew the marriage certificate.

'You brought it with us?' She laughed then, her eyes reflecting the gold of the sun filtering through the leaves overhead.

'Why not?' He pushed it away. 'It's positive proof of the conclusion of my business deal.'

Had the air turned chill, or was the drop in temperature registering solely on the scale of her happiness? 'Please stop calling it a "deal",' she said quietly. A smile crept across her still-throbbing lips. 'It's usually called the marriage vows.'

Blaze laughed and moved away, leaving her to re-button her top. 'Vows that sealed the transaction and delivered you into my keeping.'

'And they lived happily ever after.'

He turned to her, his warmth vanished. 'Is there any reason why we shouldn't?'

The cool man dismayed her. Where had the lover gone? The conversation, she realised, had taken a curious turn. Afraid to speak in case she said the wrong thing, she shook her head in answer.

He gazed into the far distance, following the line of the horizon. Studying his profile, Carla traced with her eyes the thick brows, the long nose, the uninhibitedly sensual fullness of his lips. His jaw was as firm as the character it reflected.

Unseeingly, she looked at the view, supporting herself on her hands. Blaze sat, knees bent, his hands clasped loosely. Carla found her thoughts wandering to him, feeling the need arise in her to touch him. She allowed her head to swivel slowly, gazing at his thighs, a mere finger's distance from her. Why shouldn't she follow her instincts and make physical contact? She was his wife now. Hadn't he make love to her last night without asking her permission?

Tentatively, her hand moved to rest on his knee. He looked down at it, then resumed his scrutiny of the chequerboard landscape like a chess player pondering which move to make next. Except that he seemed prepared to ponder all day, making no move at all.

Affronted, Carla withdrew her hand, but her attempt to appear absorbed by the comings and goings of walkers and picnickers, from whom they were mostly shielded anyway, soon flagged. Where had Blaze gone in his thoughts? Were they with the other women who she knew must be scattered about his life, past and present? Or was his work preoccupying him?

Whatever it was, she experienced a compelling need to distract him, to attract his attention back to herself. Again her hand moved, this time to rest on his thigh. A muscle twitched beneath her slight pressure and he turned to look down at her, eyes narrowed from the sun's rays homing in on her face. A creeping sensation brushed over her skin.

He had looked away again! Annoyance and injured pride were a volatile mixture. Her hand pulled at his arm, shaking it and tugging it hard enough to separate his clasped fingers. There was a provocative smile waiting to greet him, anticipating his laughing response.

When he turned on her, snarling, 'Is that what you did when you sent my brother crashing to his death?'

It was like part of her dying. Her smile slipped away, leaving her lips trembling, her throat thick with tears. 'What are you saying?' she mouthed. 'You're standing in judgment on me on our wedding day? Accusing me again of a most terrible crime?' The tears rose and spilled over. 'And all I wanted to do was to—to touch you and—and tell you I loved you.'

There was a smothered curse and he urged her down, twisting his body to cover hers. His lips traced the tears' path, taking them into him, smoothing her hair with near-savage strokes. He was crushing her, but she did not care. She would have given her every breath to hear, between his burning kisses, the words that had never come from his lips.

No apology came, either, nothing but a hunger for which, despite the hard, commanding pressure of his hands and the bruising possessiveness of his mouth, there seemed to be no appeasement.

At last he stopped, moving to lie beside her, cheek on cheek. Not even a tear slid down to separate them, since each one had dried and gone away. Carla's body was on fire for his lovemaking, but she would not stretch out even a finger to touch him. She could not stand another reprimand, not now, after his kisses had overlaid, if not erased, his earlier harshness.

Blaze rolled on to his side, looking her over. 'Damn it, I want you, woman.' His fingers twisted a lock of hair. 'Why didn't we do the sensible thing and go to bed, instead of coming here . . .' He moved away, finding a comb and using it, raking back his dark hair. 'Come on, we'll find an eating place and get back. I'm not waiting much longer. A man doesn't let his wedding night go by with-out——'

He left the sentence to finish itself. Hand in hand, they half ran down the hill path. Overhead, the leaves, tinted into premature autumn colours by the setting sun, brushed against each other as if for re-assurance in the face of approaching night. Birds swooped, appearing agitated, as though there was much to be done before darkness came.

Carla's senses were heightened and, like the night before, when Blaze's body had pressed against hers and they had danced, there was music in her mind. Hair blowing in the breeze, she gazed up at him, enraptured by him as her husband, her lover. His searing accusation had been left behind back there on the hilltop.

His thoughts, she reasoned, must have been on his work; the problems he must surely be presented with constantly had not been forgotten even on his wedding day. Since he could not, at that moment, direct his fretfulness about them to his colleagues, it had surfaced as an embittered taunt against her. Yes, she smiled into his eyes, she had forgiven him.

His arm slipped round her waist and hers lifted to his. Beneath her hand she felt the lean muscle, moving with his every step, and delighted in the strength of the man she loved. Now he was holding her hip, and even as they walked his fingers moulded and caressed. Moments before they emerged from the woods, he turned her towards him.

'Kiss me, sweetheart,' he commanded, and she complied, tilting her head and standing on tiptoe to reach his mouth. For him, her effort was not enough. His arms encased her, holding her the length of him, lifting her slightly and pressing her nearer until she could feel his increasing desire. His kiss left her breathless again, and the lights danced in her eyes.

'You see,' he muttered, nuzzling her neck, 'my appetite is as much in my loins as in my stomach.'

'If we don't eat,' she teased, tugging at his hand, 'you won't have the strength . . .'

'Cheeky little madam!' he retorted, his eyes throwing back the lights in hers. 'Before many hours have passed, I shall be showing you just how much *strength* I do possess. And,' he turned her face for a swift kiss, 'I won't be as gentle with you tonight. You'll learn what a man's love means.'

A man's love, not my love . . . Fiercely, she banished the doubts. Nothing would spoil her happiness, nothing! They dined beneath Tudor beams and red laterns, while candles flickered in tinted glass bowls. Flames were lit and dishes sizzled over them. Wine stood crookedly in tubs filled with ice.

Waiters came and went, Blaze drank toasts to his wife and Carla drank toasts to her husband. They laughed together, held hands across the table and Blaze's gaze, steadier than the candle flame between them, promised passion in the long night ahead.

As they walked from the restaurant in the evening air, Blaze's arm pulled her to his side. Carla shivered, then wondered why. The air had cooled only a little from the daytime temperature.

'Do you want my jacket?' he asked, going for the zip fastener.

'No, no, we'll soon be home.' 'Home', she had said. She looked up at Blaze. Yes, he had noticed.

'Home,' he repeated. 'From now on, whatever I possess is yours to share. Remember that, Carla mine.'

'It sounds like you're remembering me in your will,' she joked, and he slapped her for her impudence.

Blaze used his key to let them in. In the entrance hall he turned her, placing a kiss on her smiling lips. 'I'll see you soon, upstairs.' His glance held desire and an unspoken instruction. Get ready for me . . .

'It's too early for bed, Blaze,' she pretended to object to his silent command.

'I've waited, you witch,' she was winded as the length of him hit her, teased by his breath stroking her mouth, 'I've waited from the moment we were made man and wife. No, longer even—since the last time I made you mine, and that was nearly twenty-four hours ago. Too long, woman,' he put tingling touches around her ear, 'too long to wait to seal a marriage. Now, get up there—my bedroom. It's yours, too, now. I won't give you long.'

Carla looked around Blaze's bedroom. Large, illuminated by softly glowing wall lights, it overlooked the river. She closed the curtains on the outside darkness, too preoccupied to notice the gleaming moon-path across the water.

Never in her life had she felt so alive. No one, she considered, running a comb through her hair, could have foreseen the events that would occur as a result of her brother's excluding her from his home.

After three years of continuous recall of that hostile face which had gazed down at her in a hospital bed, the enigmatic grey eyes had watched her without a single spoken word, the condemnation implicit in his unyielding attitude. But now that had all been forgotten. He had married her, which meant he had forgiven her—hadn't he? She was here in Blaze's bedroom—his wife.

Emerging from her daydream, she heard a voice raised in shrill accusation. Opening the door, Carla listened. No need to strain to hear what was being said—it was plainly intended that the conversation should reach her ears.

Janetta Horner was angry. Oh dear, Carla thought smiling sarcastically, feeling her wedding ring with confident fingers, who had upset the beautiful Janetta? A few moments later, she knew the answer.

'Did you have to *marry* her?'

'I don't have to explain my every decision to you,' Blaze returned quietly.

'Don't you? Don't you? How many times have we——' the question seemed to choke her—'have I lain in your arms? *I'm* the one you should have married, not that scum of the river! Yes, Rolf told me what you called her.'

'Correction,' Blaze answered mildly. 'It was how she described herself.'

'Well, she was right,' was the spiteful rejoinder. The other girl's voice softened, wheedled. 'I'm on your social level, Blaze. I'd know how to behave as the wife of a top executive. You know I love you.'

'Too bad and too late.' It seemed that Blaze's patience was ebbing. 'My ring is on *her* finger.'

'After what you said, too!' All pretence at fawning had gone. 'Rolf told me. After Crispin died, you told Rolf that if you ever came across the girl who killed your brother, you'd do everything you could to make her life a misery. Admit you married her to have your revenge!'

Carla, her face drained, felt the pain of a clenched hand on the door handle. She waited for the denial that never came.

'And I know again why you married her.' Janetta's voice had gone thin and sharp. 'Because even if you'd married me, I wouldn't have wanted a child. Yes,' it was a malicious hiss, 'I've hit the target, haven't I, caught you on your most tender spot. You want a child, maybe two. When you've had them by her, you'll abandon her, won't you?' There was the coaxing note again. 'Won't you, darling? Then you'll divorce her and marry me.'

Carla sped silently along the carpeted corridor, entered her old room and raked in the wardrobe. Her own blouse and jeans hung there, cleaned and pressed. Her worn quilted jacket was beside them.

In a few moments she had discarded the outfit she had been wearing and which Blaze had bought her. Then she was back in her old clothes, her old skin, driftwood, flotsam. Blazing with defiance, her own eyes stared back. So what if she'd promised Blaze she would never leave him? That had been when she had loved him. Now, after what she had heard, that love had turned to hate.

In her earlier wanderings, she had discovered a flight of stairs to the side of the house. Ellen used them frequently in her comings and goings. They led to the kitchen area. Now Ellen and Herbert were away. She would slip out of the house unnoticed.

Only when the cool night air hit her did she realise the enormity of the step she had taken. Yet she'd had no alternative, she argued. Blaze had been going to make her life a misery, have his revenge. He'd planned to abandon her when she . . . when they . . .

Her speeding feet took her across the lawn and down to the riverside. She glimpsed her boat at the mooring, bobbing about with each slap of wave against concrete. The sound of the weir grew louder. Pushing the strap of her bag more firmly on to her shoulder, Carla pressed into the dark foliage of the bushes, hoping Blaze had not yet discovered her absence.

Since the *River Lady* was now afloat, Carla assumed that Rolf Horner had repaired the leaks. The moon's light showed her that a few of his tools lay on the benches. Crouching down, Carla extracted them, placing them on the lawn. She put a foot over the side, only to draw it back.

It was essential before boarding to discover which way the wind blew. If it was towards the weir, she would stay hidden somewhere until it changed. To her relief, it blew in the opposite direction. This meant she could drift with the current until she was out of earshot of the house. Only then could she start the motor. She kept her fingers crossed that Rolf had repaired that, too.

Carla cast off and the *River Lady* drifted downstream towards her old mooring. Catching at an overhanging branch, Carla manoeuvred the boat alongside the bank, tying the rope to a tree.

Dropping her bag, she flopped on to the hard bunk. The bubble of her wedding day happiness had burst in her face. It was just as it had been when it all began—being deprived of her job and pushed out from her brother's house all in one day. Once again, there was no roof over her head except the newly-painted one above her, no stability or security to give her peace of mind. The boat rocked as another boat drifted past. *No one who cared about her any more . . .*

There was a chill all around her, but there were no covers tucked away. She removed her quilted jacket and draped it over her. It was the same as it ever had been—except that she had changed. And it had been Blaze who had changed her, vitalising her, bringing her slowly, determinedly to the very apex of happiness.

'Determined'—yes, that was the right word to describe his manipulation of her emotions. Last night, she thought, covering her eyes, when he had taken her so tenderly, almost she had foolishly hoped, with love—it had been nothing but a smokescreen for his real feelings—complete distrust and total condemnation. How could she have allowed herself to be so misled by his kisses and his passion as to believe he had forgiven her?

Something was crunching over last year's leaves, brushing past branches and bushes. Her hearing, more acute in such a lonely, isolated situation, picked up the sounds from the river bank. Had her hideaway been discovered? Was it some official coming to tell her she was trespassing on private land?

The boat tipped and wallowed under the impact of an intruder and the door to the interior burst open. Carla pushed away her jacket, swung her legs to the floor—and stared into the ice-cold eyes of her husband.

'How did you know——?' she began, holding her throat.

'It didn't take much working out.'

'What do you want?' she asked belligerently.

'You,' was the cool reply. 'You're my wife. I want you.'

'But I don't want *you*, Blaze. You see, I heard what Janetta said. I knew you didn't love me and couldn't understand why you were so hell-bent on marrying me. Now I know.'

'You know, do you? Tell me.'

He stood before her, hands on hips, thick sweater pulled over an open-necked shirt, well-worn slacks fitting tightly over thighs and calves. He looked faintly piratical, with his hair straying over his forehead as if he hadn't bothered to comb it after changing. The moon made craters of his eyes and put grooved crevasses in his cheeks.

'Revenge,' she flung at him, 'because you still believe it was my fault Crispin died. Also, you're going to make my life a misery. What better way than to marry me, then break my——' she so nearly said 'heart', 'my spirit. Most terrible of all, you want me to bear your children,' she was whispering now, 'afterwards turning me out of your house and your life, but keeping our son or—or our daughter.'

'You've got it all worked out, have you?'

'No, but you have, and you can't refute that because you didn't deny one single statement Janetta made. Deny now,' she challenged, 'that you want me to have your children.'

'I hereby confirm,' he stated icily, 'that I intend you to have my children. But,' he moved a step nearer and his voice was spiced with malice, 'not yet, Carla mine, not until I've made your life a misery. Isn't that what you said?'

She wanted to shrink away but steeled herself to stay. There was something in his manner, a kind of unswerving resolve which made her deeply afraid. Her eyes looking up at him in the moonlight must have told him of her fears, because he laughed, throwing back his head.

'Do you think I've come to end your life as you ended my brother's? I can see the signs of terror— wide eyes, parted lips, short, frightened breaths.' He bent slightly and reached out. 'These,' he held a breast familiarly in the palm of his hand, 'rising and falling enough to drive a man mad.'

'Don't touch me, Blaze!'

Her tearing fingers round his wrist only made him hold her more tightly, moulding and pressing until her nails turned into claws with the pain his ruthless hands were inflicting.

Then she was freed from him, only to hear him say, 'I'll do more than touch you, sweetheart, before the night's out. Until now, I've played it your way— vows, legalities, ring. Now you're bound to me, I can do what the hell I like to you. And everything I give, you'll have to take.'

'So Janetta was right.' Bravely she confronted him, her face whiter than the moonlight painted it. 'How——' she choked, 'how could I ever have thought I loved you? I *hate* you now, do you hear?'

'Hate me, my own. It makes no difference.' For all his apparent coolness, it seemed her statement had angered him. He gripped her arms and urged her backwards to the berth. He threw her on to it and her back met its hardness, taking her breath.

Holding her gaze, Blaze divested himself of his sweater. With one hand he unbuttoned his shirt, freeing it from the waistband. She was fascinated by the breadth of his shoulders, his lean tapering waist. His shirt landed on the other berth, and it was then that she came to life.

'What are you doing?' she whispered. 'You can't stay here. There's no room.'

His only answer was a quirk of his eyebrow. He bent over her and pulled her roughly into a sitting position. It took a few seconds to remove her sweater. She realised then just what might be his intention.

'Get out!' she cried. 'This is my boat——' His hands were unfastening her front buttons and her own hand gripped his to stop its movements. 'No, Blaze, I won't . . . you mustn't . . .'

'You will and I must.' He jerked the blouse from her shoulders and there was little left for him to remove. When his hand went to the button on her waistband, she twisted away on to her side.

'This is our wedding night, Blaze.' There was a plea wrapped up in the statement.

'So? What do you expect me to do? Treat you like an untouched girl when only last night you let me help myself to everything you offered?'

His sarcasm hurt like a thorn in her finger. 'Last night you were wonderful. You were my lover, tender, gentle . . .'

'And now I'm your husband, about to tame my runaway wife. I'm damned if I feel *tender*, *gentle*.' He drew out the words mockingly.

He pushed at her shoulder to give him access to the hook behind her back. She was half naked and covering herself, staring up at him with furious eyes. He came down beside her, on to his side and smiling devilishly into her shocked face.

'There's not a thing you can do about it, is there?' he taunted.

Carla tried drawing away from him, only to find that her back was against the boat's side. The rocking motion he had created by joining her so suddenly was dying away.

The narrowness of the berth had their flesh touching explosively, the friction of his ribs against hers bringing about a flare of fire. The moon had moved and was shining straight across them. In its light she saw his sparking glance singeing a meandering trail across her shoulders and breasts, and quickly she covered them.

'Move your arms,' he commanded, but she gripped each of her shoulders more tightly.

His hands found her waistband again. Her lightning reaction was to stop him, but she realised at once that in attempting to do so she had inadvertently obeyed his order. Her indecision had given him the advantage and she felt the waistband give.

'Leave me alone!' she cried. 'I don't want you like this.'

'That's too bad, Carla my own. It's how you're going to get me. Wives who run away from their husbands need to be taught a lesson.'

'It's you who needs the lesson,' she hit back, fighting him with all her strength. 'You refuse to believe me when I tell you the truth about how Crispin——'

Her words were cut off by the impact of his mouth on hers. Her head was imprisoned between the hard wooden hull and the even greater hardness of his mouth. He forced her lips apart savagely, ravaging the sweet-tasting moistness, making it his own.

Her taste buds came to life, responding to the feel and taste of him. Their chemistry was mixing into an explosive compound over which he, and only he, had control. This she resented and fought against, to no avail.

A few seconds later she felt her jeans being peeled away. The rest, for him, was easy. And all the time he held her mouth hostage. Slowly her arms moved and there were jerking sobs tearing at her that he should be treating her this way.

Her hands had nowhere to go but his shoulders, and even though her nails dug, he seemed not to feel their effect. Against her thighs, there was a sensation that seemed to burn her skin and she knew again the potent effect of his nakedness.

Having achieved his object, he released her mouth and she spat furiously, 'You're brutal, you're savage . . . and this is rape. I—I can get you for this!'

'*Get me?* Your husband, making love to you on our wedding night? The champagne we drank must have gone to your head, sweetheart.' The endearment was harshly spoken. 'But I promise you, there'll be no rape tonight. You'll give and give freely.' His hands followed the line of her shape, lightly feathering, knowledgeable of a woman's physical reactions, yet extracting the greatest pleasure also for himself.

When his palms stroked her breasts and his mouth skimmed her shoulder, Carla held her breath in delight. The moment his lips teased the hardened points and her body arched towards him, her reasoning mind knew he was right. She was giving willingly, rapturously. When the moment came for him to take her, she could have sworn that among the whispered endearments she heard him murmur, *I love this woman* . . .

CHAPTER SEVEN

AFTERWARDS, they lay for some time in each other's arms. Carla thought Blaze was sleeping. The berth was narrow and when she moved slightly to ease the pressure, he opened his eyes. The moonlight slanted across his face, showing that he was too alert to have lost consciousness.

Her hair was spread out and his cheek anchored it to the pillow. His head lifted and he took a golden handful, twisting it tightly. He tugged and she told him he was hurting, but he did not release it.

Instead, he pulled her with it close enough to fit his mouth over hers. The kiss delved and held no tenderness. Even with his conquest of her body, it seemed his anger with her persisted. His intention was plainly to arouse, and in this he succeeded at once. Carla felt a throbbing longing deep within her and knew the ache would go only when he took her.

He had no intention of taking her. He ended the kiss abruptly and pushed her away. His body swung from the berth, leaving her skin creeping with cold—and with total shock. He couldn't be leaving her like this, ready for him, pulsating for his love . . .

'Where are you going?' Her voice came at him out of the semi-darkness as he dressed, pulling at the zip on his slacks.

'Back to civilisation. Where else?'

'You mean you're going, walking out on me, just like that?'

He raked her with his gaze. 'Shouldn't you cover yourself?'

Carla was glad he couldn't see the colour stain her cheeks. How much more was he going to humiliate her? He turned to the pile of her clothes, scooped them up and dropped them, item by item, along her white body. It was a mocking gesture, coloured with contempt.

He was at the cabin door. Only then did he answer her question. 'Yes, I'm walking out on you. You walked out on me, so why shouldn't I reciprocate?' His mouth curved sardonically. 'See you around some time.'

The boat rocked as he stepped off. The crunch of his footsteps taking him away made reality of a nightmare. Until then, Carla had thought he was fooling. Even in his absence he dominated the small cabin cruiser. Still she felt his body exciting hers, his mouth robbing hers of its quiescence, leaving behind the havoc of his searching, inflaming kiss.

The tears came slowly, slipping down to the corners of her mouth, acting as a salve to the bruises his lips had inflicted. She had had to run, hadn't she? Blaze hadn't denied, even to her, a single word of what Janetta had said. Knowing she had overheard, how could he treat her as if *she* had wronged *him*?

Well, she knew it all now—he had begun his campaign of revenge. In this one act alone—by possessing her and then discarding her—he had already started to 'make her life a misery'. And children? What if a baby resulted from their two nights of lovemaking?

In a swift, rejecting movement she was off the berth and pulling on her clothes. The consequences, loving Blaze as she did, were too terrible to contemplate.

Until dawn Carla lay with her eyes closed, and only when the chorus of birds began did she slip into a brief, refreshing sleep.

The sounds of the other boats on the river awakened her. Children running up and down the opposite towpath, within call for the first meal of the day, reminded her forcibly of the night's events. The sun rose on a sparkling day, but Carla's eyes were dulled with the pain of dismissal by the man she loved.

The aroma of numerous cooking breakfasts drifted

across as she stood watching the scene. The water was so still it mirrored the trees' reflections to perfection. Long-branchéd willows swept low, like fingers reaching to dabble. Lombardy poplars stretched high and majestically, admiring their own reflected images.

Flowers put lines of colour, like an artist's touch, to the edges of the lawns of other riverside houses. Even the weir's sound was softer, as if the sun had muted its roar. There was a special river smell which seemed to arise, not from pollution, but a mixture of water and fresh air. Over the past weeks it had seeped into Carla's system like a tonic.

Even now, in her sadness which, after being wrapped in Blaze's arms, should have been unbounded delight, it invaded her spirit, uplifting it. The world was awake around her and going its own way undeterred by the gaze of a young woman who, despite the rings on her fingers, began to feel that she belonged to no one.

She began also to feel the gnawings of emptiness. Her mouth longed for liquid, but there was not a drop of fresh water, nor a single tin of food on board. This meant a visit to the shops in the high street.

Finding a comb in her bag, she pulled it through her hair. There were cleansing pads tucked away and these refreshed her face. Anxiously, she hoped the motor would behave. To her relief, it started first time and she silently thanked Rolf for his diligence. Making her way across the river to a vacant mooring, Carla secured the boat.

Until she entered the grocery store, she had forgotten that her purse was as empty of money as her pockets. Since her arrival at Blaze's house she had

had no need for cash; he had paid for everything. Now, she had no alternative but to go to the bank and draw on the pitifully small amount which was left in her account. It was, she remembered, almost down to single figures.

Her possession of Crispin's engagement ring had always been at the back of her mind. As her savings had decreased, so the ring had come to represent not merely a symbol of reassurance, but an encashable article which would ensure that she was provided with the basic necessities of life.

Now it had gone, and she had to face the fact that every tiny amount she withdrew from the bank took her nearer to the brink, to that dreaded 'rock bottom'. She fingered the diamond ring which Blaze had given her, but she would rather die than sell that.

The counter clerk willingly supplied her with a note of the entire amount the account held. Carla studied the scrap of paper, hardly daring to read the figures scribbled on it. She held her breath and re-read the amount, then she smiled ruefully.

'You must have misread my account number. I don't have this amount in mine. I only wish I had!'

The girl frowned, compared numbers and assured Carla that the account number was certainly correct. The amount written on the slip of paper was hers.

Carla shook her head bewilderedly. 'But I don't have a three-figure bank balance. It *must* be a mistake.'

'Just a moment, Miss Howard.' The girl went away, then returned. 'A Mr Blaze Douglas paid a cheque into your account three days ago. At least, the cheque was signed by him, drawn on his account in another bank.'

Carla turned a fiery red. She could not rage at the counter clerk, saying, 'Mr Douglas is my husband and I don't want my husband's money!' Nor could she say, 'Send it back.' There was only one thing to do. She would draw out the minimum amount to see her through until—when? The divorce? The thought gave her a physical pain.

One day, she told herself, when she had a job and was able to live an independent life, she would repay every bit of that loan—she refused to look upon it as a gift. As she stepped down into the boat, lowering the heavy shopping bag, the anger had not left her.

If only she had been able to throw the money back at him! Added to what had happened between them last night, and his walking away as if—as if he had *used* her, the discovery of the money was an insult, a humiliation she would not easily forget.

Having eaten and tidied up the boat, she gazed around, her eyes coming inevitably to rest on the weir. It was empty of anglers at that time of day. There was a way on to that narrow walkway across it and she decided to find it.

Crossing the river by the bridge, she joined the towpath, noting that most of the moorings were free, the holidaymakers having moved on. Walking with care along the narrow bridge, she clung to the handrail. Turning her back on the great white house she had come to know so well, she stared down.

The water foamed and danced over elongated steps, leaping again as it frothed whitely on meeting the grey-blue river. In the warm sun, the weir seemed almost benign, holding none of the terrors which stormy nights bestowed on it.

Turning, Carla rested both arms along the rail and looked at the house from which—was it only yesterday?—she had escaped. Her wandering eyes stopped abruptly as they came upon a figure staring back at her. His hands were in the pockets of his jeans, his long legs slightly apart. His shoulders were back, his head up, and he looked every inch the lord of the manor.

How had she first regarded him? Carla wondered, trying vainly to slow the rapid beat of her heart. Remote and unreachable? Despite the fact that he was now her husband, and that they had spent two nights in each other's arms, Blaze was still the unreadable stranger she had first glimpsed staring down at her after the accident.

'Heartless and without pity,' Crispin had called his brother. How right Crispin had been! Hadn't she accused Blaze of it herself?

Even as their gazes locked, she felt the urge to reach out with her arms—but kept them firmly at her sides. Why should she be the one to plead forgiveness when it was he who had wronged her? He turned his back on her and made for the house, disappearing from sight.

He had left her watching his retreating figure, but what else could she have expected? You're the most unscrupulous and pitiless man I know, she had told him not so long ago. *You'd do well to remember that*, he had replied. She had started to forget and was paying the penalty. To him, revenge might be sweet, but to her it held a bitter taste.

*

For a long time after she had stretched out on the berth, Carla listened for the crackle of footsteps on the bank. She hoped—how much she hoped—that he would come to her that night.

Sleep overtook her determination to stay alert. When daylight came, she stirred to immediate wakefulness, only to discover that he had not come. Throwing off the rug she had bought the day before, she satisfied her small appetite with breakfast cereal and wheatbread.

That afternoon she went into her home town about five miles distant to find a job. 'Nothing today,' the smiling agency employees had told her. They could afford to smile, she thought acidly. They were safely behind office desks shaking their heads at hopeful, if increasingly hopeless, people.

Having nothing else to do, she scrambled out on to the bank and stood there, wondering. She looked at the greenery, the brambles beneath her feet, and remembered the land belonged to Blaze. *You could always go back*. The words crept stealthily into her mind. That, she scolded herself, was the very last thing she would do!

After her meagre evening meal, she remembered Blaze's sarcasm, the day after she had arrived, about her simple tastes. She recalled Ellen's concern about the small breakfast she had asked for. The memory returned also of the way Blaze had kept upsetting her and how concerned the doctor had been about Blaze's 'sharp tongue'. There was that moment when Ellen had come in with the tray and rushed to comfort her after Blaze's harsh accusations.

Knowing all this, why had she allowed herself to

become entangled to such an extent that she was now his wife? It was then that she realised just how clever he had been in his dealings with her.

All the same, she told herself hopelessly, she loved him, always would, even if they drifted apart—a cir= cumstance brought all the nearer by her act of running away from him. And he seemed to be in no hurry to get her back. Was it all part of his campaign to make her life a misery?

For a while she read a book she had bought. The evening sun was sinking, sparkling orange-gold through the tree branches, bringing a faint shiver along her uncovered arms. Going inside for her jacket, she pulled it on, taking her shoulder bag with her. There was a path through the trees on the bank which was part of Blaze's land. It led past the boat club and up to the bridge.

The walk she took was a long one, past the moored boats from which music came, and raised family voices. All the canopies were in place, keeping the weather and the night insects at bay. Here and there through a 'window' came the flicker of pictures on portable television screens.

Arriving at one of the busy locks which punc- tuated the many miles of the Thames, she watched as two or three boats entered. When the lock gates came slowly shut, Carla admired the rows of care- fully cultivated flowers which lined the lock's sloping banks. The boats were on their way upstream, probably looking for empty moorings.

It was almost dark when she reached the path to her own boat. She, too, would pull the awning into place, then read for a while before going to bed. Pushing aside the final bush which hid her boat from view, she stopped dead. Someone had been—and gone. And that 'someone' had madly, frenziedly, smashed her boat to pieces.

For a moment she could not move. Shock had frozen her to ice, her blood-flow was log-jammed by it, her heart enmeshed in it. A blind fury began the melting process and she came to life, running towards the remains, going on her knees and reaching down.

Pieces of driftwood—*driftwood*—floated where the cabin cruiser had been. The tartan travelling rug had caught on a branch. Then she saw that it was just part of the whole, the rest had been ripped to pieces. Tins of food had sunk to the river bed, their labels, having become detached, floating brightly. Packets lay soggily, partly scattered over the bank.

Stretching down, she picked up a board which, by its comparative neatness, seemed to have been hacked purposefully away. '*River Lady*', it said, and she wanted to cry. Still holding it, she rose, feeling shaken by the force of her heartbeats. Only one person called her River Lady.

Blaze—he must have done this. Another of his ways to make her suffer, another act of bitter revenge. She threw down the wood and started to run. The fury had intensified, carrying her through the tangle of bushes, balancing her when she tripped over jutting tree roots.

If she had to wait all night, she would confront him, denounce him. She did not care who heard. Her feet slowed to a stop. She cared if he was out and Ellen or Herbert came to the door. There would be explanations, protestations, appeals on their part for her return. This she could not face.

The tall, wide gates to the rear of the house were wide open. This indicated that Blaze was indeed away from home. Maybe, after the satisfaction of depriving her of her only roof over her head, he had gone out to celebrate. His car was missing, the garage door open.

Hiding in the bushes, Carla paused to consider the situation. In no circumstances was she going back to his house. There was another place she could shelter. Herbert had mentioned it in passing and only yesterday she had seen it from the footbridge over the weir.

Separated from the main building, yet next to it, was a boat-house. Behind the trellis-like doors she had seen a small boat, just a little larger than the *River Lady*.

Creeping over the gravel, she cursed the way it crunched beneath her feet. Somewhere a dog barked, but she knew it belonged to someone else. All the same, it startled her as she continued on her way. At last she was past the house and straining her eyes to find the rear entrance to the boat-house.

The moon, which had risen into a clear sky, helped her in her quest. The doors creaked as she unlatched them, closing them behind her. Crouching down, she read the boat's name. *Cape Horner*, it read, and for a few seconds she smiled. The boat belonged to Rolf and, as with all other boats which came his way, his tools were spread everywhere.

Stepping carefully into it, Carla found her way inside. It was better equipped than her own boat had been. The past tense brought her back to reality and her hand went to her head. She flopped hopelessly on to the berth, and, weary beyond words, went straight to sleep.

'Hey, what's this lost lamb doing here?' Carla's heavy eyelids lifted. Surely it wasn't yet time to get up? Darkness all around, except for the beam from a hanging latern indicated that the night was still in small hours. At the end of the light-beam stood Rolf in the entrance. He looked as if he had hurriedly pulled on some clothes.

'Sorry, Rolf,' Carla mumbled, putting shaky feet to the floor and swinging her long, tumbled hair from her eyes. 'There was nowhere else to go.'

He frowned, considered, then shook his head hopelessly. 'I'm lost. Put me in the picture, ma'am.' He attempted to joke as he stepped into the interior of the rocking boat. He suspended the lantern from a hook in the roof.

'Why did you come down here, Rolf?' It was her attempt to divert his mind from the subject.

'I heard my neighbour's dog bark, so I got up and listened at the window. There were suspicious noises. I knew I hadn't locked those doors,' he indicated the boat-house entrance from land, 'and since this boat is mine I came to investigate. The last thing I expected was to find you here.'

He sat beside Carla on the bunk. Carla knew she would have to explain, but there was no way in which she could bring Janetta's name into it.

'Blaze and I—we quarrelled, and I—I walked out on him. You see, I heard——' She looked at him. No, not even now could she tell Janetta's brother what she had heard Janetta say.

'A rumour?' Rolf hazarded. 'Someone told you what Blaze said the night Crispin died?' She nodded. 'That if he ever found that girl again—and he was going to make it his business to do so—he'd make her life hell. He had a plan—he never told anyone what that plan was.'

I could tell you, Carla thought miserably, rubbing her tired eyes. It was to find me, marry me, then start tearing my life to pieces. Just as he ripped *River Lady* to pieces. She looked around.

'Why does Blaze allow you to keep your boat in here, Rolf?'

'Because my boat-house is full up with my new boat. Blaze owns a sea-going yacht—he keeps it way down-river. I'm getting this little cruiser in shape to sell.'

'You've bought a better model?' He nodded. 'More expensive?' Again he nodded, and Carla smiled. She had heard the story somewhere before, but for the moment the time and place eluded her.

'Like Crispin used to better his women. I was his best friend, do you know that?'

'He—he thought I was a "better model" than the girl he'd had before me?'

Rolf nodded. 'I know he'd given you an engagement ring, but he would never have married you, Carla. Having a fiancée kind of upgraded his status. Know what I mean?'

'And he had a girl he could call on whenever he——' she looked at Rolf uncertainly, but continued, 'whenever he felt the urge.'

'Right, Carla.' His glance was questioning.

'Well, all I can say is that he had unlimited patience. I never once——'

'He told me he was going to ditch you if you didn't deliver the goods on the night of his birthday.'

She looked at him quickly. 'Is that true? Did

anyone ever tell Blaze?'

'Seemed to be no point. Crispin was—wasn't around any more.'

Rolf did not realise how great a weight he had lifted from his companion's shoulders. To be free of that haunting feeling of guilt—that her action of breaking off their engagement had given rise to the fatal accident ... All she had done was graze Crispin's pride by making the break first! No wonder he had decided to get drunk.

The lifting of the weight, she thought sadly, made no difference to her present situation. She sighed deeply and Rolf's arm went round her. There was the touch of lips on her hair, but she did not reprimand him. It was probably the only sympathy she would receive where her present plight was concerned.

He was fingering her rings and she felt him trying to tug them off. Snatching her hand away, she looked around, seeking another diversion. 'This boat,' she remarked, then breathed in, 'it smells, Rolf. Is it—is it oil?'

He laughed. 'It's B.O.—boat odour. It should really watch the television ads!'

Together they laughed, Carla's laughter carrying on beyond Rolf's. Her breath caught, then she burst into tears. Her face turned to his shoulder and he held her, both his arms going round her.

'What's wrong, honey?'

'Oh, Rolf, you don't know what's happened. *River Lady*—she's been smashed to pieces!'

Rolf had stopped breathing. Carla could feel it. 'Not——?'

'Blaze—it was Blaze, Rolf. Part of his plan to per-

secute me. He knew where I was. He found out—
well, a long time ago, where I moored my boat.
This evening, I was so miserable, I went for a long
walk, right up to the next lock. When I came back, it
was nearly dark, and *River Lady* had been flattened.'

Tears ran unchecked down her cheeks.

'So you came here.' She nodded. 'Why didn't you
go home?'

'Home?' she echoed bitterly. 'I haven't got a home.'

Rolf lifted her chin and placed a light kiss on her
forehead. 'You could come with me, share my——'

'She'll share nothing of yours!' The voice rang out
from the entrance to the boat-house. Blaze strode
down the steps and his weight tipped the boat omin-
ously.

'Hey, Blaze,' Rolf stood up, alarmed, 'don't sink
my boat as well as——' He looked at Carla.

'As well as breaking *my* boat to pieces!' Carla
cried, running to the cabin entrance which was
blocked by Blaze's solid form.

He stepped down into the cabin. 'Rolf, do you
know anything about this?'

Rolf lifted his shoulders noncommittally. 'Why
should I know?'

Carla's hands reached up to Blaze's shoulders and
she tried to shake him. 'Don't try to blame someone
else when *you* did it—*you*! It was part of your strategy,
wasn't it, to harass me, torment me. Don't try and
deny it!'

He brushed her hands off as if they were stray
hairs. 'So I won't try to deny it. You said it.'

Tears rushed to her eyes again, she could not stop
them, but she did not seek her husband's arms to cry
in as she had sought Rolf's. Don't weep on my

shoulder, he'd called to her that night she had first tried to moor at the end of his garden.

'So you did do it.' Her lips trembled. 'How could you, how *could* you?' She seized his arms and tried shaking those. He merely shook her off. 'I said once before you hadn't got a humane bone in your body,' she accused, turning away and pressing her mouth. She turned back. 'Rolf?' Her voice was defiant. 'Can I take you up on your offer? Go with you to your——'

'Rolf?' Blaze's voice was sharp.

'Okay, I'll make myself invisible. Carla, any time.' His eyebrows rose, asking, do you understand? She nodded and he sprinted up the steps and away.

Blaze jerked her towards him. When she touched his body, alarming sensations chased through her. Please, oh, please, she thought, make love to me. One tender gesture on your part would make me forgive you, even though you wrecked my boat. You see, I love you so. Can't you feel my pulse tripping over itself at the feel of you?

The words that came from her uncaressed lips were completely at odds with her thoughts. Her mind whispered, he thinks ill of you, won't listen when you say you were innocent of causing Crispin's death . . .

'What are you going to do now?' she attacked, picking a snap of defiance from the rubble of her emotions. 'Whatever it is, you won't break my spirit like you've broken *River Lady*!'

He thrust her away, pocketing his hands in creased brown slacks. His white rollnecked sweater was dazzling in contrast to his storm-dark eyes, his dark hair unruly. He stared down at her in the light from the lantern.

'Blaze,' she said sadly, 'why? Why did you even have to rip up my new blanket and tear my book to pieces? Do you hate me that much, Blaze?'

His jaw firmed. She had not even disturbed the surface of his humanity. Although, she argued, how could you touch something which didn't exist? He turned on his heel and climbed outside, making the boat rock again.

Carla found her shoulder bag, then reached up to extinguish the light from the lantern. He was waiting to padlock the door. Uncertain now, she awaited his next move. Ignoring her, he walked towards the house, his pace fast, and Carla found herself running to keep up with him.

He let her in through the side door and walked into the house. At the foot of the stairs, he turned.

'Your things have been moved back to your old room. Unless, of course, you'd like to spend the rest of the night in Rolf Horner's arms. Goodnight.'

He did not even look back to see if she was following.

When Carla went down to breakfast, Ellen and Herbert were delighted to see her.

'Have you come back to stay, Mrs Douglas?'

Mrs Douglas! Was it really true? She looked at her rings for confirmation.

'For—for a while,' she answered. 'I mean—' at their startled expressions, 'yes, yes, I have. What happened was that I—I——'

'Well now,' Ellen interrupted firmly, plainly closing her mind to any unacceptable action on the part of an ecstatically newly-wedded woman, 'it looks like I must start feeding you up again.' She shook her head. 'You've let yourself go thin again, Mrs Douglas.'

'Food, Ellen,' Carla laughed, 'is that your remedy for all ills?'

'No, my dear,' Ellen replied, ever reasonable, 'sometimes it's the cause of "all ills". In your case, not to mention your dear husband—' 'my husband', Carla thought, astonished, 'who for some strange reason has been off his food, too, a few good nourishing meals will work wonders.'

'Would it improve my temper, Ellen?' Blaze's amused voice came from the door. Carla turned, her heartbeats already racing as though a starting gun had been fired. He was dressed for the business world. His pale blue shirt contrasted well with the grey material of his suit.

To Carla's weary eyes he looked altogether too handsome and she was in danger of falling even more deeply in love with him, if that were possible. If only he hadn't made that savage attack on her boat!

'I'm beginning to doubt if anything will ever do that, Mr Douglas.' A quick glance at Carla, then, 'I was hoping marriage might mellow you, but——' Ellen shook her head.

Blaze's amusement did not last. His eyes were cool as he motioned Carla to a chair at the breakfast table. 'Why don't you join me, darling?' he asked, mockery glinting in his look. Ellen appeared to suppress a smile as she placed prepared halves of grape-fruit in front of them.

Carla wanted to call to her, Don't go, Ellen. I've got nothing to say to this man you keep calling my husband. But Ellen bustled away.

Carla picked up her spoon and attacked the loosened segments. She could find nothing else on which to vent her pent-up anger. Blaze had erected a newsprint barrier which fenced in his mind as well as his face. You couldn't, Carla reflected wryly, fume at headlines which talked so blandly and so intellectually back at you. If only Blaze read one of the more chatty tabloids . . .

I'm angry about so many things, she told herself—about my restless night, about his smearing innuendo about my sharing Rolf's bed, about my boat. This hurt most of all. She supposed it was because of what it represented—an escape route, a symbol of independence and, if she wanted it, freedom.

Carla glared at the unresponsive printed pages across the table. Freedom was the last thing she longed for. If only she could batter down the paper barrier, shout to her husband that her love for him bound her more tightly than any tangible bonds.

She sighed, knowing that even if she reached out and struck at those eminently reasonable columns of fact blurred by opinion, she would only find another, and more formidable, barrier beyond that.

When Ellen carried in the main breakfast course, Carla thought, At last he must put away that newspaper! He merely folded it, placed it by his table setting and continued to read it while consuming his meal. Carla stared at her overflowing plate trying to clear her misted eyes.

Unexpectedly, Blaze spoke. 'Anything wrong? Aren't you hungry?'

Refusing to let him see her unhappiness, she seized her knife and fork. 'Very,' was all she replied, without raising her eyes.

It was as she poured her second cup of coffee that Blaze shot back his cuff to consult his watch. In one fluid movement he was on his feet. At that precise moment, the door bell chimed. Blaze frowned and as Herbert could be heard greeting the caller, the frown deepened.

Rolf appeared in the doorway of the breakfast room. 'Hi, Blaze, Carla.' He was in leisure clothes and looked fresh and eminently sure of himself. To Carla he seemed oddly familiar, and she put a hand to her head. At the moment of his appearance, she had experienced a flash of *déjà-vu*.

She stood up, disliking the way her personality was diminished by the presence of these two totally confident men. It hit her as she rose—the almost palpable tension in the atmosphere.

'What do you want, Rolf?' Blaze's manner was so abrupt Carla looked at him.

'Hell, Blaze,' Rolf answered, 'I'm not having an affair with your wife just because I offered her a roof over her head!'

'So that was all you were offering her, was it?' Arched eyebrows said the rest. Rolf's jaw thrust challengingly. Blaze's return strike was to make his adversary witness his departure.

He crooked his arm towards Carla and smiled, and at once she went to him. In her delight at his invitation she missed the fact that, despite the curve of his lips, his eyes stayed stone cold.

His hold was like the bars of a human cage. His kiss held the craving hunger of an imprisoned man. Without inhibition, he devoured her answering kisses, yet, still unsatisfied, came back for more. She clung as if her time with him was rationed—then he let her go. She stared up at him, infected now with his insatiable desires.

She knew what it was like to be the one who was left behind. Neatly, cleverly, he had padlocked the gates—leaving her inside.

He strode to the door, nodding to Rolf, and Carla felt as if he had torn the very heart from her and taken it with him.

CHAPTER EIGHT

THERE was a long silence, broken only by the sound of Blaze's car driving away. 'For crying out loud, Carla,' Rolf exclaimed, 'why did you have to marry the man?'

Carla could only stare at him.

'*I'd* have married you—and loved you. That miserable swine will only make your life hell.'

Still Carla stared. This was another Rolf Horner, one that had her pulses drumming like a warning in the jungle, portending evil.

'Didn't Crispin ever tell you about his big brother?' Rolf went on.

'Often. He said he was heartless and had no pity.'

'He was right, Carla, believe me. He nearly beat the life out of Crispin when he got engaged to you. Well,' he qualified, 'verbally. Said you were——'

'Too stupid, too shallow. I know, because Blaze told me.'

'*Blaze* told you?'

Carla nodded. 'But I knew he was opposed to the

engagement.' She started stacking the used dishes. She added bitterly, 'I don't know why Crispin didn't tell his brother the engagement was only a sham, a way of getting me to——'

'Isn't it obvious? Crispin wanted Blaze to think he'd already——'

'Got me. Male pride and all that.' She was silent, leaving the dishes. It came to her that she was in danger of hurting another male's pride. She looked up. 'Thanks for what you said just now, Rolf.' She tried the soothing ointment of a smile, and it seemed to work.

'I meant it, Carla.' He came round the table. 'Last night on my boat, I wanted you, darling.'

Something inside Carla recoiled at his blatant manner of expressing his desire. 'I'm married, Rolf.' This time the smile exacerbated the wound. His eyes glowed, not with sorrow, nor with understanding.

'You'll be telling me next you love the guy!'

Carla just prevented herself from nodding. There was a recklessness about Rolf that eddied beneath his smooth surface. Then he visibly relaxed—the professional salesman in him appeared to take command—and his smile was coaxing.

'I called to ask you out again. I've got the day off before I go abroad for a week. So come on, honey, keep a brokenhearted guy happy for a few hours.' His hand settled over his heart. 'If I can't have your love, I'll make do with your company.'

Carla was laughing as Ellen came in. The housekeeper looked sideways at Rolf. 'Hallo, Mr Horner,' she said. 'You're an early visitor.'

'He's got the day off, Ellen. He wants me to go out with him for an hour or so.' Carla glanced outside. 'The sun's shining. It won't hurt me, Ellen, will it?'

If she had thought her question would appeal to Ellen's motherliness, she was mistaken. 'Does Mr Douglas know, Mrs Douglas?' Was her emphasis on her newly-acquired name a means of reminding its owner of her marital status? 'He doesn't? Well, all I can say is, it might hurt *him*.' Ellen marched out, the tray stacked with rattling dishes.

'She never did like me,' Rolf commented, smiling ruefully. 'She used to say I was a bad influence on Crispin. It never occurred to her to turn the situation the other way round.'

'From what I've heard,' said Carla, 'I'd take a guess the two of you were as bad as each other.'

'Thanks, pal. You must have thought a lot of Crispin.' The touch of acidity reached her.

'I really meant as *good*.' Her smile was brilliant. She knew she had won him over when he reached for her hand.

Rolf drove to a local car park, and they walked along the high street, looking in the shop windows, and having coffee in a small café where the air was heavy with freshly-baked bread. Carla drew some appreciative breaths, and, having settled the bill, Rolf bought bread rolls warm from the oven. These were filled with savoury meats of their choice.

'We'll have a picnic, okay?' Rolf said, and Carla, wishing the man beside her would change magically into her husband, nodded.

They strolled along the towpath across from the bank which was lined with houses of varied styles, both neo-Gothic and modern, painted in all colours. Blaze's house, Carla thought with pride, shining bright as it was, looked the best of all.

'We'll go for a row,' Rolf decided, taking Carla's agreement for granted. He handed her the small carrier bag containing the food and paid an attendant for the hire of a boat.

He stepped into the rocking wooden vessel, as accustomed to the rolling movement as a moorhen to riding the wash from the continuous coming and going of pleasure boats.

Carla found stepping into the shallow boat more disconcerting than into her old cabin cruiser. Hurriedly she sat on a hard seat while Rolf manipulated the long oars with ease. He pulled on them, manoeuvring first with one, then the other, turning in the direction in which he wanted to go.

This, Carla saw, was past Blaze's house—she still could not look upon it as hers, too. Rolf rowed with skill, but as they neared the weir, her fears grew.

'Please, Rolf,' she urged, 'I don't like the weir.' Its sound was loud enough for her to raise her voice.

Rolf laughed, and the light of small-boy devilment switched on in his eyes. He took the boat nearer and watched her tightening hands. 'Still too near?' he enquired, grinning. He used an oar to turn directly towards the speeding waters.

'No,' she pleaded, 'no, no!'

His grin widened as he let the boat drift with the river's current. It was taking them to—who knew what? Carla thought with desperation. The consequences of going over the top could, she had heard, be fatal. Was this to be her fate, and Rolf's too?

His eyes, which reflected back a twisted version of her own desperation, frightened her. His words brought her near to screaming pitch. 'I can't have you in life, so why shouldn't we be joined together in the next world?'

'What are you talking about?' The shriek verged on hysteria.

With an ease born of a boyhood's experience of the river's moods, Rolf reached out for one of the posts forming a warning barrier to boats which had ventured too near. He had had the situation under control all the time!

'Why, you miserable fraud!' she shouted at him over the weir's roar. His laughter rang out, fiendish and tormenting. 'You gave me the fright of my life!'

Not quite, she amended silently. If only Crispin had had his car under the same control as Rolf had this rowing boat—how differently life would have worked out for her, then. But Rolf's head had not been muddled by drinking too much alcohol. The action, however, had, she was certain, been motivated by something else, but it was beyond her to discover the answer.

Carla could not fully enjoy the remainder of the journey. She did not smile, nor did she speak. Her eyes functioned, even if her brain had taken refuge from the storm roaring through her emotions.

Cabin cruisers passed continually, some small and cosy, others a little larger to accommodate families. Her trailing fingertips felt the soothing quality of the water, her lungs drew in that fascinating air-and-water river aroma.

The greenery was everywhere. Trees lined the banks, climbed local hills, shedding their varying leaf shades and greening the grey-blue water with their own reflections. There was peace and happiness all around, but it could not find a way into her heart.

Mooring the boat, they ate their rolls and drank from cans which Rolf had bought. Rolf talked and laughed a lot and Carla found herself joining in, but if anyone had asked her to repeat what Rolf had said, she could not have done so.

Leaving the boat, they returned to the car, on the way crossing the suspension bridge and feeling again the throb of the traffic which passed over it. Rolf reversed the car—long and low as Crispin's had been—and drove with Crispin's abandon. Where were they going? she asked, trying to sound interested. Towards Oxford, he told her.

I want to see Oxford with Blaze, not with you! She almost blurted out the words, but she contented herself with a sigh.

'It's not been a success, has it?' said Rolf, shattering her composure.

So he had noticed . . . 'I've enjoyed the day, Rolf,' she answered, 'really I have.'

He stopped the car, reversed it and returned in the direction from which they had come. 'We're going back. You're as sick as hell with my company.'

Treat him like the small boy he's become, her reason told her. 'You're wrong, Rolf. Of course I've enjoyed your company. Blaze—Blaze has never taken me on the river or picnicked with me, like you have.'

Her tactics seemed to have humoured him. He would not have liked her thoughts if he could have read them. Why had the day seemed so long? She knew the answer. She had spent most of it wearying for Blaze, which was why she had had such a restless night.

Blaze had not come. If he had, and had taken her in his arms, telling her he was sorry to have wrecked her boat . . . A man like Blaze would never apologise, she admonished herself. She was still telling herself that fact when Rolf swung into the grounds of the Douglas residence.

'Okay, get out,' Rolf said sulkily.

'Oh, Rolf, haven't you enjoyed the day just one little bit?' She caught his hand and gazed into his eyes.

A reluctant smile took away the sullenness, and two seconds later he had pulled her into his arms. Carla was stretched awkwardly across the controls and receiving a passionate kiss. When she was finally able to ease herself from his embrace, her hair was ruffled, the neckline of her sleeveless dress out of place.

As her hands lifted to tidy her hair, she saw out of the corner of her eye a larger, sleeker car drawn up beside them. Its driver was staring at them, tight-lipped and coldly angry. Carla stared back. Did Blaze really think she was capable of initiating such a kiss as Rolf had given her?

Blaze slammed out of his car and strode towards the house. 'Go on,' Rolf jeered, 'run after him and go on your knees for forgiveness, like the obedient little wife you are.'

'I'm sorry, but I love him, Rolf. I hate hurting him——'

'He didn't hate hurting you when he broke up *River Lady*, did he?'

'All right, he doesn't love me in return. And he married me out of revenge, and because he wanted to make my life a misery, and because——' She could not tell him, or anyone, how she felt about having Blaze's children.

'How do you know all this?' Rolf demanded, eyes sharp and questioning.

'I overheard Janetta talking to him the day he and I were married.'

'I warned you she was out to get him.'

'I got him first, didn't I?' She was out of the car and speeding towards the house before Rolf could answer.

As she burst into the house, Ellen appeared. 'Where's Mr Douglas, Ellen?' Carla asked, breathless.

'Gone upstairs, Mrs Douglas. I warned you he wouldn't like you going out with Mr Rolf, didn't I?'

'It was all very innocent, Ellen. All we did was walk and row on the river and picnic.'

'I believe you, dear, but——' Her eyes moved upwards, casting doubts on whether her employer would believe his wife.

'I'll explain,' Carla called back, racing up the stairs. Outside Blaze's bedroom, she stopped. Afraid her courage would go if she hesitated for one second, she burst into the room. It was empty, but the sound of running water came from the bathroom.

Creeping towards it, she discovered that he was not in the bath, which meant he must be under the separate shower. Since no one could conduct a conversation in such a situation, she began to back away, but a hand came round the door and tugged her into the room. He had seen her reflection in the long mirror!

The wet hand fastened round her wrist and she was pulled inexorably towards the shower curtains.

In a moment Blaze's veiled outline turned into flesh as she was propelled forward through the break in the dripping curtains. He jerked her against him, his smile full of malice undiluted by the water which ran from his face.

His hair was flat, his chest hard, the muscles of his legs and arms even harder. She was imprisoned against him as she had been earlier that day, but this time his mood was harsher.

'My clothes,' she cried, 'they're soaked! How could you, Blaze? I——'

His mouth cut off the explanation she would have made. His hands pulled at her dress, unzipping it and taking it off. The rest of her clothes joined it and her bared flesh throbbed as it was pressed against him.

He reached behind his back, but she was too far gone into his kiss to wonder what he was doing. A lightning-flash later, she knew. He had turned the shower to 'cold' and she was shrieking in protest.

'No, Blaze, no!' The cascade of icy water was a shock to her system and she cried out again, fighting for breath. He showed no mercy, covering her mouth until she started sinking to her knees. He let her go, and she stayed there, clinging to his legs, her cheek against his hip, filling her lungs with the air he had denied her.

Again he pulled her up. His mouth roamed, starting at her throat and moving down to her breasts. When his tongue caressed the hardened pink-tipped circles, she held him to her, her ecstasy unbounded. Straightening, his hand fastened on her hair, its red-gold darkened by the water. Her head was jerked back and his mouth covered hers again.

He turned off the shower and his arms lifted her out, yet still the kiss persisted. He lowered her to her feet, releasing her lips at last. With long, strong strokes he dried her back and front, then throwing aside the towel, he carried her through the door and dropped her on to the bedcovers. The feel of him beside her, his leg thrown across her, made her body burn for him. Her skin, already stinging from the lash of the freezing water, was quivering for his touch. He did not disappoint her, but first he turned her chin roughly and stared into her eyes.

'That's what I do when my wife spends the day with another man, and gives a "thank-you" kiss when he brings her home. If you ever slept with that double-dealing neighbour of mine, I'd thrash you until you came crawling to me for mercy. Get it?'

Holding her eyes, she nodded, then slipped her longing arms around his neck. Blaze moved on to her and caressed every part of her pliant, desire-racked body, then he took her and her joy was complete.

Next morning she awoke alone, but in Blaze's bed. Smiling, stretching luxuriously, she recalled their laughter over dinner, his open admiration of her emerald satin gown, their discussion of his work.

He had never before talked to her as his equal, never treated her with such warmth. She wondered if he had at last forgiven her for the part he was convinced she had played in Crispin's fatal accident.

At bedtime, she had gone upstairs first, having lingered for the invitation to share his bed. It had not come, and she had gone to her lonely room despondent. It had been impossible to sleep. Memories of their encounter under the shower, and Blaze's subsequent lovemaking, kept returning both to plague and please.

It must have been about one o'clock in the morning that her door was opened and Blaze stood there, gazing down at her. The light from the landing must have shown him that her wide brown eyes were staring up at him. Had they contained hope, or even invitation?

Whatever it had been, he had swept the covers from her and lifted her, taking her to his bed.

'I want you,' he had said, 'I can't sleep without you.' He had parted her lips and drunk from the honey-sweetness of her. Her body had arched against him, and their passion had flared once more.

Now, satiated, she lay gazing through the net curtains at the cloudless sky, wanting to stay where she was until night-time came again, afraid that if she left Blaze's room the memories would follow her out and be lost for ever.

It was in the late afternoon that Carla heard a car arriving. It was too early for Blaze to return from work, so she did not stir. She lay in the garden, having sunbathed for much of the day. Sometimes, she had sat in a garden chair and read a book. Now and then her attention would stray to the busy river, watching the rowing boats and the cabin cruisers go by.

Her eyes had lifted to look at the exact spot on the opposite towpath where, until two or three weeks ago, she had stood every evening for a month and stared across at this house. Now she was a totally different person. Her future happiness was assured—wasn't it?

Blaze must have forgiven her for that crime she had never committed. She had certainly forgiven him for smashing up *River Lady*. One day she would have to contact Derrick, whose boat it was, and offer to pay compensation for its loss.

A woman's voice drifted from the house. 'You surely don't mean Blaze and his wife have separate rooms, Ellen?' High-pitched laughter followed, giving Carla the final clue to the puzzle of the visitor's identity.

Sitting up and pulling a jacket over her strapless sun-top, Carla started the countdown to the explosion of her anger. She had forgotten—and Blaze had not bothered to remind her—that when Rolf went away his sister Janetta stayed at the Douglas residence.

As Blaze's wife, shouldn't she have been consulted? She should have known her mood of intense happiness would not be allowed to last. How stupid she had been to believe that Blaze had 'forgiven' her. A man could make love, passionate love, without 'love', couldn't he?

'Having a lazy time, *Mrs* Douglas?' The feline quality of the inflection and the choice of words was as abrasive in its effect as the speaker had intended.

Janetta lowered herself gracefully on to the other garden chair. Carla, cloaking her irritation, affected a sweet smile. 'You may call me Carla, Janetta.'

The angry flush in the visitor's cheeks gave away her feelings, yet she inclined her head with graciousness. Carla envied her her poise.

For a while Janetta contemplated the scene, not with appreciation for its tranquillity, as Carla had done, but with an air of dismissal of the ordinary families in small, cramped cruisers.

Carla, withdrawing her eyes from the girl's classic profile, felt sure that this seductive female knew what it was like to sail with Blaze in his sea-going yacht. The thick, dark hair, the cream silk embroidered blouse and slacks tailored to perfection, spoke of unerring fashon sense and the income with which to indulge it. It told also of the personality to back up the wearing of clothes bearing famous name-tags.

No wonder Blaze appreciated his neighbour's sister and allowed her the freedom of his house whenever she wished. The question was—had Janetta Horner the freedom of Blaze's bedroom? Maybe, just maybe, she had in the past. *Now he was married, would that freedom still be granted?*

Carla broke the silence. 'Has Ellen given you a comfortable room, Janetta?'

The girl's head turned slowly. 'There's no need to play the lady of the house with me. I've been around here a darned sight longer than you.'

The visitor's rudeness, Carla determined, would not go unchallenged. 'Yes, Blaze told me how you make use of his house every time your brother goes away.' And she can take that how she likes, Carla thought uncaringly.

Janetta stood up, facing Carla. 'Look, *Mrs* Douglas, I know you're now the wife of Blaze Douglas, but don't count on it, will you, that he'll stay faithful to you for ever and a day? Because,' her teeth snapped together, 'I intend to make it my business that he and I resume our relationship—our very intimate relationship—the moment the opportunity arises. And I'll make sure that opportunity arises very, very soon!'

Carla followed her swaying, slender figure into the house. The front door opened and Blaze was eyeing them both. He nodded to his guest. 'Janetta. Of course, Rolf's away.'

'You don't mind, darling, do you?'

'Mind?' Blaze appeared puzzled. 'Of course not. Why should I?'

'Because your sweet young wife here hasn't exactly been the essence of politeness to me.'

Carla smiled at her husband. 'Janetta has quite misunderstood, darling. I asked if her room was comfortable. I said I knew you welcomed her to your house at any time.' With an even sweeter smile, she hit Janetta's acrimonious glance right back over the net.

Blaze looked quizzically from one to the other.

Janetta gave him a seductive smile. Carla ran to him and threw her arms around his neck. 'I'm so glad to see you, Blaze. I've missed you all day long!'

His smile was a crooked affair as he kissed her parted lips. 'Happy to see you, too, Mrs Douglas.'

A small pleat on Carla's forehead signified a certain puzzlement. Which of us is play-acting? she wondered bewilderedly. Blaze stooped and kissed the frown away.

'I must wash off the cares of the business world,' he stated, releasing his wife and striding up the stairs.

'Point to you, Mrs Douglas,' the visitor snapped. 'But you can't dispute the fact that *you* ran to him!'

Janetta smiled a brittle smile, turned and stepped on each stair as if it were made of candyfloss.

Over dinner, Janetta sparkled. She seemed to have decided that the meal was to be a formal one. Her dress was a pale yellow, framing her face with its upstanding collar, then pointing down to a low neckline. The skirt was ankle-length, the belt a shiny silver to match her jewellery.

Carla's simple deep-blue shirt-waister, with its short-sleeves, made her feel like an under-privileged guest invited to the host's table out of pity. This, she reflected, was probably Janetta's intention. There was no doubt, either, that Blaze's attention was more drawn to Janetta than to his wife.

Janetta's clever conversation made sure of that. They were discussing the subject they both knew best—that of office equipment and business systems.

'This exhibition you're holding soon,' Janetta was saying, causing Carla's head to lift from the food she was forcing into her, 'where will it be, Blaze? In the usual place—the conference room at Head Office— your Head Office?'

Carefully, she distinguished between his company and the one for which she worked.

Blaze pushed away his empty plate, leaning back and hooking his arm over the back of his chair. 'This year, Janetta, it will be here, in my house.'

'My' house, Carla noted, discarding her unfinished sweet course. She could not subdue the involuntary look of surprise as she raised her head, to find Janetta smiling as if she had won a fortune.

'Don't you discuss your work with your wife, Blaze darling? You really should have told her how *your* house was going to be invaded by hordes of business men of all shapes, companies and languages.'

Blaze glanced lazily at Carla and the blood raced

in her veins. 'I didn't want to bother her beautiful head with matters of business on what should really be her honeymoon.'

'Our honeymoon.' The correction slipped out and Carla could have kicked herself. The comment received the smile from their guest which she knew from the moment she had spoken would come her way.

Blaze bowed ironically. 'Our honeymoon, my love.' His attention returned to Janetta. 'The change of venue was made since I now have a hostess to welcome the guests,' his narrowed eyes slewed again to Carla, 'a beautiful woman by my side,' his hand reached out to take hers in his, 'one, moreover, I've promised to love and cherish until——'

'Until another even more beautiful woman comes along. Isn't that correct, Blaze darling?' Janetta's smile was brilliant, her eyes like imitation diamonds. 'By the way,' she executed a neat change of subject, but one nonetheless which kept the limelight on her, 'while I'm staying with you will you have your usual quota of typing for me to do?'

'There's plenty,' Blaze answered succinctly.

'Do you share Blaze's office?' Carla asked, with seemingly idle curiosity. She was glad Blaze could not see the turmoil in her heart.

Janetta's answering smile should, Carla felt, have been accompanied by a purr. 'Yes, Carla, I do,' she answered. 'Now that should set your teeth on edge, shouldn't it?'

Blaze looked faintly amused, but did not speak. Ellen entered with the coffee tray.

'Here or over there?' she asked, indicating the living-area. Blaze replied with a nod and the housekeeper carried the tray to lower it on to a glass-topped table.

They moved across and Blaze stood by the couch. Carla hesitated a fraction too long, and Janetta occupied the place she herself had almost taken. Blaze seated himself next to his guest, while Carla was forced to sit alone in a deep armchair.

Again Janetta took the initiative, arranging the coffee cups and pouring the coffee. She stopped in mid-pour, a finger to her mouth like a small girl who had done wrong. 'I'm so sorry, Carla. This is really your job now, isn't it? But I'm so accustomed to pouring for Blaze——' she shot a sly, sideways glance at him, 'to acting as his hostess, in fact, that I did this automatically.'

She offered the coffee pot to Carla, who could only invite her to carry on. With her head on one side, Janetta appealed to Blaze. 'Am I forgiven, darling?' He moved his hand, indicating that she should continue.

And continue she did, all evening, dominating the conversation until Carla grew so restive she rose, telling Blaze that she was going to bed. On impulse, she bent down to kiss him and he gave her a smile so full of promise her heart sang.

'Blaze darling,' Janetta said before Carla had reached the door, 'tell me about the work you have for me.'

As Carla climbed the stairs, she heard them making for his office.

It had been a hard decision—which bedroom should she go to? After their lovemaking of the day before, and the night she had spent in his arms, there would have been no hesitation on her part, had Janetta not been staying there.

This, however, was the factor which had pushed her towards Blaze's room. As his wife, she had an undoubted right to sleep in his bed. Now, having showered and put on her most seductive nightgown, she lay waiting for him to join her.

When an hour had passed, she told herself not to fret, since she had come to bed early. Another hour of waiting stiffened her limbs and tensed her mind. She must have drifted into a light sleep, since whispered words woke her.

'Come into my room, Blaze, like you used to do,' Janetta was coaxing. 'What does a piece of paper matter? You know yourself that you married her for the children I wouldn't have.'

'Janetta, we have to talk.' Blaze's answer was a little louder, but beneath the firmness Carla was certain she could perceive acquiescence. As if to confirm her suspicions, a door was closed and there was silence.

'No, no,' she moaned, then hid her face in the pillow, breathing deeply to conquer the threatening tears. Rolling at last on to her back, she began to analyse the situation with her reason, letting her feelings retreat into hiding.

If Janetta had manipulated Blaze with such ease such a short time after his wedding, and—Carla could hardly bear the thought—within hours of his making love to the woman he had married, then what was she doing here, waiting tamely for him to come to her?

No doubt, as he made love now to Janetta, he was laughing at the thought of his compliant little bride waiting in vain for her bridegroom to come and kiss her back to life . . . Her legs swung to the floor, she seized her wrap and crept outside, listening. Then, in her bare feet, she raced along the corridor to her own room.

Even as she closed the door she heard whispered words—endearments, no doubt, the sweet-talk of lovers who knew each other's needs and satisfied them liberally, with maturity and total lack of inhibition.

Wandering to the window and watching the now-silent river beyond the garden, she wondered sadly how she could ever have thought she could please a man whose appetites went way beyond anything a novice like herself could satisfy.

In the quiet darkness, she slept, awaking reluctantly to an overcast morning. With her still was the sensation that something had walked into her dream, stood beside her for a long time, then vanished. Her sleep-filled eyes had opened sufficiently to tell her that the 'something' was tall, male and commanding, but before she had had time to reach out with her arms, sleep had tugged her back from the brink of consciousness.

CHAPTER NINE

By the time Carla had gone downstairs for breakfast, both Blaze and Janetta had left for their respective work places.

The day seemed extra long and when Carla grew tired of sitting on the lawn, she wandered inside. Blaze's office door stood open and Carla, with a small twinge of conscience chased away by a shot of defiance, walked in.

Posters still lined the walls, but they had been added to. There were pictures promoting instant filing systems, equipment with screens and keyboards, even vending machines with a large range of liquids on offer. The many and varied offspring of electronic engineers' minds made her dizzy. Did the inventions of technology have to look so impersonal and cold?

A thought made her smile wryly. Was that why Blaze was like that—as cool, remote and enigmatic as the equipment his company promoted? Carla wandered to a desk. It was a simple, understandable affair, made of wood, with a grain that registered on her fingertips. It had drawers, too, which opened when she pulled.

The best thing about it was that it had no buttons to press, no coloured lights that flashed on with each and every one of the operator's thoughts. It must, she reflected, have almost reached antique status among the business systems of the future but which seemed already to have started their take-over bid for men's minds.

On the desk stood a typewriter, large, heavy and, of course, electric. This must be the machine Janetta used when she helped Blaze with his work.

The door was pushed open and Janetta came in, coming to a surprised stop.

'What are you doing in here?' she demanded. 'Spying on Blaze's company secrets?'

'I might ask the same of you,' was Carla's commendably cool reply. Inside, she was furious at the other girl's proprietorial attitude.

'I'm here to use this.' She indicated the typewriter. 'Didn't you hear me ask Blaze last night if there was any work for me while I was here? It's the way——' she paused, eyeing Carla spitefully, '*one* of the ways in which I pay for my bed and board. Now, will you excuse me, please?'

Janetta went to the typewriter and made a show of busying herself with folders, and Carla went away, wondering which of them had won that mini-skirmish.

The day had been long, but the evening seemed longer. Carla had decided to emulate Janetta in dressing for dinner. She wore a dress which moulded to her full-shaped figure. Round her neck she draped a matching stole, encircling her throat to drape backwards over her shoulders. The colour was palest pink which, instead of clashing with her red-gold hair, enhanced its rich shade.

Blaze was staring through the patio doors, a drink in his hand, as she entered. He turned and subjected her to a thorough, male scrutiny.

Carla gazed at him across the room, the pendant earrings she wore as still as her breathing. She was waiting—waiting for a word of appreciation, and she could not disguise the fact. It did not come, and she chided herself for behaving like a garden bird waiting for the tablecloth crumbs to be shaken on to the lawn.

'Have you dressed for me, Carla mine?' was Blaze's sarcastic question. 'Or was it a gesture intended to get even with our guest?'

Affronted by his derision, she snapped back, 'I'm not "yours", nor would I dress for a husband who spent the night with his house guest!'

He put down his empty glass and advanced slowly. He stood close, hands in pockets, head back, eyes hooded. 'You've just made two serious accusations, my own.' His jaw moved, signifying a simmering anger. His hands whipped free of the confining pockets and fastened bruisingly on her upper arms.

Carla willed the protest to stay in her throat, enduring the pain rather than let him see her distress.

'One, you are indisputably *mine*. Two, produce the evidence to support your contention that I slept with Janetta.'

Spoken so bluntly, the statement made her wince. 'I heard you——' she moistened her lips, 'heard you both talking. She—she invited you into her room. I also heard you go in.'

'So you ran from my bed like a wounded rabbit and wriggled into your burrow to nurse your injuries.'

'Please let my arms go. You—you're hurting me, Blaze!'

In response, his hold tightened and he pulled her the length of him. Carla wanted nothing more than to rest her head against his broad chest, to nestle up to him and be kissed back to happiness.

Nevertheless, she flung back her head and challenged, 'Did you expect me to lie there like a dutiful wife awaiting your pleasure after you'd finished making long and passionate love to your woman?'

To her astonishment he threw back his head and laughed. His hold slackened. 'If I had made long and passionate love, then come along to "my dutiful wife", I would have needed to be made of the stuff of which superman movie heroes are made to have satisfied *her* considerable appetite, too!'

Carla tore away from him, nursing her arms, rubbing at the scarlet marks which would turn into noticeable bruises.

Blaze's hands linked around her waist and she was against him again, his cheek against hers. I'll weaken in two minutes if he doesn't stop, Carla panicked. Then she remembered that they would not be dining alone.

'I came into your room in the early hours,' Blaze was saying softly. 'You were asleep, but you stirred and whispered my name.'

Carla turned pink. Had she really called to him? She would not concede victory! 'Prove it,' she used his words, 'produce the evidence that you came into my room.'

'Check,' he answered, eyes glinting as he let her go. 'You think you're clever, don't you? Well, I'm a step ahead, my love. You'll never "checkmate" me. Next time you separate yourself from me, I shall wake you up. Would that be proof enough to suit you?'

Janetta paused in the doorway, taking in the intimate scene. Her laughter tinkled like a wine glass ringing. 'How sweet!' she purred. 'And how *pretty* you look, Carla.' She uttered the ego-reducing adjective with intent. 'Me——' she glanced down at her simple summer dress, 'I look nondescript beside you. Never mind, dinner here is usually an informal affair, isn't it, Blaze? Maybe, under your tuition, your wife will learn exactly what is correct to wear for appropriate occasions.'

Her look at Carla was a waiting one, listening for the blurted-out words, But last night *you* dressed up!

Instead, Carla smiled. 'Any meal where my husband is present is a special occasion, Janetta.'

Blaze laughed, his eyes appreciative. 'Quick-witted as well as beautiful! What more could I want?' He shot a provoking sideways glance at Janetta, but she rallied with a too-bright smile.

'What more indeed?' she answered, but as Blaze turned to stand by his seat at the table she gave Carla a poisonous look.

It was after coffee that the long evening began. Janetta started the discussion in which she knew Carla could not join. Ellen came in to gather the used cups. She smiled at Carla, then looked with withering disapproval on the visitor.

Janetta warmed to her subject, which again was about their mutual interest, work. Blaze listened. There was no doubt that she had caught his attention. Carla managed to suppress a yawn and Blaze, who this time sat beside her on the couch, smiled down at her. When his arm went round her and his hand made contact with the flesh of her upper arm, she could not suppress a shiver of pleasure.

His hand began a rhythmic massage, up and down, as if to rub away the soreness he had inflicted earlier. The caressing movement, the rough feel of his jacket against the bare skin of her back, was bringing Carla's desires to stirring life.

All she wanted to do was to put her forehead against his neck, pushing into the solidity of him, hanging on to his arm as if it were a safe mooring in a rough sea. Instead, she had to content herself with a swift, revealing upward glance. His eyes lowered briefly and intimately to rest on the glimpse of her breasts which the low-cut dress allowed.

'I need advice, Blaze darling.' Janetta's words were spoken jerkily, and with the sole intention of breaking up the silent lovemaking. This she succeeded in doing, and Blaze's arm was removed from his wife's shoulders. 'The work you gave me—some of it I can't understand.' Her hand stretched towards him. 'Come with me, darling, and give me some help.'

Blaze ignored the hand but rose, smiling down at his wife. 'We won't be long,' he promised.

It was a promise he did not keep.

Next morning he had gone to London, Ellen told Carla. 'He's got a place there, an apartment or something. It's a conference, he said, something to do with this exhibition he's having here next week.'

Carla nodded as if she had known all about it, but Blaze had not said a word. That night she had slept in her own room. He had not left Janetta's side the entire evening, and Carla had fretted until she felt ill. When she went up to bed early, there was no doubt in her mind as to which room she should use.

All the same, she stayed awake for hours, hoping that he would come to her again as he had the night before. He did not, and she had awoken heavy-eyed with crying.

As she had gazed at herself in the mirror, she told herself that she knew the score—marriage to her out of revenge and for the family she would give him. So why had she made herself look terrible by crying half the night away?

When Ellen greeted her that evening with the words, 'Only one for dinner tonight, Mrs Douglas. Mr Rolf's back, so Miss Janetta's going home,' Carla could have shouted for joy. Ellen smiled at Carla's unconcealed delight, but added,

'She'll be coming for her things on her way back to her brother's house.'

Carla's mouth turned down and Ellen laughed. 'You can take her on, Mrs Douglas,' she asserted, 'and beat her hands down. You've got what she wants, dear, didn't you know?'

'As if it could have passed me by, Ellen,' Carla replied, her mood changing.

'Sorry to interrupt.' Janetta had entered quietly, using the key she appeared to have to the front door. 'I've come for my things.'

Carla was in the living area when Janetta reappeared, holding a suitcase and an overnight bag. These she lowered to the floor, as if freeing herself of encumbrances in advance of a mental brawl.

'You won't keep him,' Janetta declared pugnaciously. 'I'll fight you with everything I've got. I'll break all the rules, but most of all, I'll break your hold on him.'

Carla's brain reeled as if from a body-blow. Nevertheless, she hit back, 'Thanks for letting me know I've got a hold on him. And for telling me your tactics in advance. I'll let you into a secret, Miss Horner.' Carla looked down at herself. 'I've got everything you've got, right down to basics.'

Janetta sneered, 'It's what you do with "the basics" that counts, isn't it? I've been the female in his life for a long time. I know his needs, and I can satisfy them. I have experience on my side.'

'That's one of my weapons, Miss Horner. I'm fresh and new—still something of an unknown quantity, even to my husband. I have that elusive but essential thing called "mystery". When a man knows a woman as well as you allege Blaze knows you, the seventh veil has gone, hasn't it? There's nothing left to discover.'

Janetta seemed to find it difficult to speak. Her scarlet cheeks and brilliantly hard eyes revealed her inner fury. 'You'll see,' she muttered, 'I'll win, you'll lose!' She grabbed her baggage and walked out.

Ellen put her head round the door. 'Well done, Mrs Douglas. I told you Miss High-and-Mighty Horner had met her match in you!'

Exhausted from the encounter, Carla sank to a chair, holding her head. 'I wish I had your confidence, Ellen. All I know is, the fight's going to be a hard one.'

Rolf rang after the evening meal. 'Come for a drink with me at the Boat Club?'

Carla thought, why not? Her spirits were low, she was missing Blaze, who had not even called her on the telephone. 'I'd love to,' was her answer.

They arranged a time and Rolf, spirits plainly higher than Carla's, said, 'When the master of the house is away, little wifey will play.'

'If you're going to be like that, Rolf——'

'I'll be a good boy,' he answered, laughing, and rang off.

When Carla told Ellen she was going for a drink with Rolf Horner, Ellen frowned. 'You ought to keep away from those two Horners, Mrs Douglas. They're not saints, either of them, are they, Herbert?' she called to her husband, who stood in the kitchen door. 'Mr Crispin and Mr Rolf were friends and they got up to all sorts of tricks together.'

'They were much younger then, Ellen,' Carla reminded the housekeeper gently.

'It wasn't their age, was it, Herbert?'

'It was their nature,' Herbert agreed. 'Mr Rolf hasn't changed much, for all his getting a bit older.'

'All I can say, Mrs Douglas, is what I said before. Mr Douglas won't like you going out with Mr Rolf.'

'Don't worry, Ellen. I'll deal with my husband when he comes home, whenever that is.'

'More likely he'll deal with you,' Ellen muttered.

Rolf was charm itself as they sat at the bar in the main lounge of the Boat Club. The building was a large, converted house and everywhere the visitor looked there were photographs of boats—large, small, yachts, canoes, catamarans. There were flags of different countries, of clubs; crossed oars adorned walls, models of ancient sailing ships stood on shelves.

Leaving the club house, they wandered down to the river. It was almost dark and Rolf groped for Carla's hand. At first she resisted but then, convincing herself he meant no harm, allowed him to hold it. He took this as a sign of encouragement, however, and pulled her round to face him.

Her hands went up in a gesture of self-preservation, pushing against him, but he reached over to her mouth and kissed her. Again she thought, it's just a testing kiss on his part to see how far I'll let him go. She was pulled against him then. His kiss grew more audacious and she tried the pushing action again, but it only made him more determined.

A cruelly biting hand on her shoulder prised her away. The other sent Rolf staggering backwards. He was within two feet of the river when he found his balance. His bottom lip thrust out and he pushed back his hair with both hands.

'I'll get even with you, Blaze! No one pushes me around without——'

'No one mauls my wife about and gets away with it. Now get away from here, before I have your name erased from the list of members.'

'On what grounds?' Rolf asked nastily.

'Assaulting my wife,' Blaze answered.

'Assaulting? Hardly. She came like a lamb when I beckoned.'

'Well?' Blaze's cold eyes inspected her. Carla shook her head. How could she explain, without appearing naïve, that she was sure Rolf meant no harm? 'I——'

Rolf grinned malevolently at Blaze and walked away.

Blaze and Carla walked separately along the road back to the house. Ellen let them in and her worrying eyes darted from Blaze to his wife. I told you so, was their message.

In the living room, Carla sank to the couch, but Blaze remained standing. 'Did—did you make all your plans for the exhibition, Blaze?' she asked.

'Most of them.' He crossed the room and got himself a drink, then walking back, he stood in front of her. 'In view of the frequency with which you go out with my neighbour——' *Our* neighbour, she thought. Have you still not admitted me into your life as the woman you married instead of just an instrument of revenge? 'Am I to conclude you're having an affair with him?'

'Don't be stupid!' Her wide eyes were shocked.

'He meant no harm back there at the club.'

'Rolf Horner always has a motive.'

'What's his motive where I'm concerned?'

'To get you away from me.'

That makes two of them, Carla thought wryly, sister plus brother. Aloud, she said, 'No one could do that. When I married you, I made the usual promise—to be true to you. I always keep my promises.'

'Even to my late brother Crispin?' Blaze tossed down his drink, putting aside the glass. He still wore the suit, with its immaculate fit, in which he had gone to London. It made him more magnetic, yet more remote. She wanted to tear down the barriers between them.

She answered his question. 'I made no promises to Crispin. An engagement is a kind of testing period. If you don't suit each other, you break the bond. You may like to know that I broke the bond. I'd told him at that party that I couldn't marry him.'

'Which is why he drank so much. Why didn't you tell me this before? Because you were afraid it would confirm that you were to blame for the accident?'

'I was *not* to blame! Anyway, Rolf told me Crispin would never have married me. He worked out that it might make me more willing——'

'I know the rest,' he cut in. 'So you broke the engagement. But didn't return the ring?' His eyebrows were lifted sardonically.

'How could I?' she cried, aroused by his intentional needling. 'He'd died!'

'With your help.'

She stood up. 'Don't you ever forgive or forget?' She shook her head hopelessly.

'You're admitting it at last?' He grasped her shoulders. 'That's all I want you to do—come clean and admit it.'

'Tell a lie to satisfy your twisted sense of justice?' she stormed. 'I'll never do that, never!' Her head dropped at the hopelessness of it all. 'I could keep accusing you of smashing up my boat, but I don't.' She waited, but there was silence. 'I'm going to bed.' Her head lifted defiantly. 'Alone.'

She left him watching her.

She was in bed face down when he came. He switched on the light, and her head turned away from him, leaving her hair streaming over the pillow. His hand reached down and felt the dampness the tears had left.

'Turn on your back,' he commanded.

'Why should I?' There was a thickness in her voice.

'Because I tell you.'

Reluctantly, Carla turned, unwilling to let him see the extent of her distress. As a defence mechanism, she tried sarcasm. 'The big boss image even in the bedroom!'

'How would you have me act—like a groping, self-effacing fool, begging for your favours?'

Her eyes found his but could not read them. Blaze reached down and pushed away damp hair. A finger flicked at a stray tear, then drew a slow, diagonal line from shoulder strap to the separation of her breasts. He wore a robe as if he had just showered.

Sitting on the bed, he pushed aside the shoulder strap, easing the fabric down until her breast was revealed. He caressed its fullness, then lowered his head, teasing with his teeth until she gave a small scream. He lifted his head, smiling at her smile. He seemed satisfied that he had banished the tears.

With a lazy movement he pulled down the whole top of the nightgown, moving from one pouting shape to the other, caressing with lips and hands until she cried out with pleasure. His arms slid beneath her and she was carried to his own room.

On the bed, he stripped her as if impatient of material barriers. He had already discarded his bathrobe. Carla felt his fingers trailing her stomach and gasped on an intake of breath. The stroking lowered to her thighs, arousing her desires until she was clinging to him and crying out for him to take her.

He was on her then, and time stood still. Only the throbbing beat of her heart went on—and on, until the golden cloud was reached and they rocked in each other's arms.

After that, a pattern was established. Blaze's bedroom became hers, there was no question about it. They made love, they slept, then made love again. Carla was treading cloud and above it the sun was always shining.

It was during the lonely days that she became uncertain. She was beginning to wonder, only to wonder, if their lovemaking had borne fruit. With his passion and his physical need of her, had Blaze succeeded in starting the family he wanted her to bear him?

If so, how many more children before he said 'Enough. Get out of my life so that I can take into it the woman I really love and want?' Then she told herself that it was too soon, that she was imagining things—but she had taken no action to prevent such a happening, after all.

In the evenings, Janetta still came to the house, disappearing into Blaze's office. For two hours or more there came the tapping sound of Janetta typing. Sometimes Blaze would join her, then there would be the sound of talking and occasional laughter.

Every time Janetta left to walk back to her brother's house, Blaze went with her. They would stand in the doorway while Janetta wished Carla happy dreams, then looked adoringly into Blaze's face. Her final smile at Carla would carry the message, I'm winning, can't you see?

Sometimes there would be a longer delay before Blaze returned, and Carla would fret, cover her face and whisper, I don't know, I just don't know.

One evening near to the presentation of the exhibition, Blaze stayed longer at the office in the town. When Janetta came into the living area before going home, she sat elegantly on the arm of the couch, displaying her long, slacks-covered legs.

Her hand came out, palm upwards. 'He's there,' with her other forefinger she indicated the centre of her palm, 'all I've got to do is——' she made a squeezing motion, 'and he's mine, then I'll break up your marriage.' She paused, for greater effect. 'Just like I broke up your boat.' It was, to her, the master stroke, and she waited for the astonishment that duly came her way.

'*You* broke up my boat? But it was smashed to pieces!' Carla eyed her opponent's slenderly-built form. 'Where did you find the strength?'

'Strength wasn't necessary. The hull was little better than matchwood—Rolf told me when he repaired it. So I knew it wouldn't be difficult, and,' with a reminiscent smile, 'it wasn't.'

'I blamed Blaze!' gasped Carla.

'I know. I laughed when I heard. That's why I did it—to cause trouble between the two of you. But although you now know the truth, if you told him I did it, in an attempt to get even with me, he wouldn't believe you.'

Carla lifted her shoulders. If she told Janetta, He never believes anything I tell him in my own defence, it would merely add one more to her score of victory smiles.

Janetta eyed her. 'Blaze makes love to you, doesn't he? I can see it in your face—the proverbial radiant bride. But *why* does he make love to you? Not because he loves you, I know that for sure, but because——'

Involuntarily, protectively, Carla's hand went to her midriff, and Janetta's eyes brightened. 'Ah! It won't be long now, will it?'

Carla jumped up, outraged but managing to contain. 'Get out,' she said quietly, 'just get out of this house.'

Janetta stood, picking up her bag. She seemed surprised at Carla's unfamiliar assertiveness. And, Carla wondered, as Janetta turned to go—just a little afraid?

Rolf telephoned often, always at midday when he knew Blaze would be at work.

He said, when Carla protested once, 'If your bossy husband keeps you in harem-like conditions, at least where I'm concerned, he surely can't object to your speaking to me like this. I mean, I can stretch out my hand, but it's the twisted flex of the connecting cord I touch, not a curling tendril of your hair.'

Carla laughed and he went on, 'You see, I'm still poetic, especially about you.' There was a change of tone. 'Darn the distance between us! I want to make love to you—hell, someone's coming. Ring you tomorrow. Okay?' Before she could answer, he had gone.

As the exhibition approached, display stands and tables were delivered to the house. These were followed by office equipment which, to Carla, looked as if they had stepped straight out of Blaze's posters and become three-dimensional. In that form, they seemed even more bewildering.

The answer to every office problem appeared to be in that large room, yet to her unprofessional eyes, would seem to add to those problems. It would surely need a high level of intellect and scientific understanding to operate some of these things.

Carla mentioned this to a man who seemed to be overseeing the delivery, the precise placing of each space object, as she laughingly called them.

Blaze overheard her words. He had, to her surprise, arrived with the man, who was introduced as an employee of Blaze's company.

Blaze put his arm around her waist. 'With a little tuition, even you could operate many of these things,' he claimed.

The telephone rang and her radiant, upward-tilted face clouded.

'Mrs Douglas!' Ellen sang out from the hall. 'Mr Rolf for you.'

Blaze frowned. 'What does *he* want?'

The engineer, called Bill, went steadily on with his work.

'He phones me most days,' Carla stated as dismissively as her anxiety would allow. 'Please excuse me.'

Aware as she was that every word she said could be heard by her husband, Carla's conversation with Rolf was stilted. He tried to make her laugh and succeeded once.

'Something wrong?' he asked after a pause.

'Yes. An audience.'

'I get it. Well, that's it. 'Bye for now.'

Blaze had been standing a few paces away. 'So you talk to him in code. All those secrets between you can't be spoken aloud in public. The "public" being me, of course.'

'It's not like that, Blaze.'

He swung from her pale, frowning face and strode back to the ballroom.

The reception took place under a sunset-painted sky, with the first stars shining palely, losing some of their brightness to the strings of multi-coloured lights which had been strung through the trees lining the lawn.

Small boats clustered, their occupants emerging to watch the mingling guests, the tables groaning under the weight of food, the elegant evening gowns worn by wives or girl-friends. Candle flames streaked obliquely in the gentlest of breezes, wine bottles popped and gushed into crystal glasses.

Carla, captivated, felt almost as if she were one of those river onlookers, cut off from the conviviality, gazing with longing, as they were doing in their hired boats.

Yet here she was, part of it, yet apart. There was Blaze, immaculate, unreachable in his formal dress, his strongly handsome face listening with a half-smile to a guest. His eyes swung unexpectedly, settling on his wife, and she met his speculative gaze uncertainly.

Was there something wrong with her dress? She had chosen it with care. It was narrow-strapped and black, the low neckline just resting across the beginning of the swelling shape on which his brooding glance lingered.

The skirt hem touched her ankles, the dark shade brought to life by the bold splash of embroidery in turquoise and peacock blue stretching diagonally from midriff to hem. She had so wanted Blaze to be proud of her, but there was no telling at all how her appearance was registering on his brain.

He spoke a word to the guest and made his way through the throng to his wife's side. 'So pensive, my love.' He lifted her chin. 'Where did you go?'

Carla gestured. 'Out there, with those people, on my boat again, looking on.'

'Driftwood, my river lady? Can't you escape from the river's call? You're no onlooker, Carla. You're here, my wife and my hostess. You should be mixing, socialising, my best and most irresistible saleswoman.'

Carla lowered her lashes, looking at him through them. She smiled impishly. 'Your best employee and your worst paid?'

'You little minx!' His fist brushed her chin. 'Know your place, Mrs Douglas, which is——' he checked himself. 'I won't elaborate. But it doesn't include being impudent to the boss. Now come on, you're the most valuable asset I've got. Get to work on some of these men—the ones without their wives,' he added dryly, 'make them drunk with your charm and they'll buy every bit of equipment they can lay their hands on.'

'Kiss me first,' she whispered, pulling him down by his shoulders. He was startled, then obliged, and her lips clung to his as if they would never kiss again. The action surprised her as much as Blaze. It was impossible to identify the source of the feeling which impelled her to make the request. She was left with a niggling sense of worry, but this she cast aside as she followed Blaze.

The introductions were many, some repeated, some fresh. Carla joined in the laughter at the jokes, followed highly technical conversation with a frown which made the knowledgeable beings around her laugh at her.

When food was offered, she ate, when drink passed by she took a glass, but she restricted these to two. All the same, there came from nowhere a floating feeling, not from the intake of alcohol, but as if, in spite of her husband's encouragement, she was still on the outside looking in.

Putting down her glass, she looked around. For a moment she was alone. Wandering into the ballroom, she basked in its emptiness. The technology which stared back at her had no life of its own; it needed human beings with the brains and the know-how to make it come alive. It was a comforting thought.

There was a movement from behind a free-standing electronically-controlled vending machine. Her eyes scanned the words, 'Coffee, Tea, Sugar, Chocolate.' Her mind was registering other things— such as the sight of Rolf shooting from a crouching position to his feet and easing his way between the machines to face her.

CHAPTER TEN

'WHY are you here?' she whispered. 'He works for a rival company,' Blaze had said.

'Just making sure everything's in working order.' Rolf's smile was oddly strained. 'Thought I'd do an old friend a good turn.'

Relieved, Carla nodded, then something tugged at her mind. He looks ill at ease, she thought. What's the matter with him? She stared at his round, flushed face and it started changing. It wasn't Rolf at all— it was Crispin.

It was three or more years back. They were at that party—yes, there was the clinking of glasses, the laughter, music—no melody now, only harsh, raucous sounds that made her hold her head. Crispin was coming towards her. He was speaking, his mouth making grotesque shapes.

Yet it wasn't Crispin, it was Rolf, there were tools in his hand, screwdriver, spanner . . . Why, *why*? *He looks like Crispin* . . . Why hadn't she seen the resemblance before? Maybe she had. That *déjà-vu* she experienced not so long ago—it had been trying to tell her. And the boats he bought, each one a more expensive model, just like Crispin and his cars.

His teasing the day he had taken her rowing, going so near the weir that she had cried out in fear, yet knowing she was afraid of it.

She had to run, she had to get away. Turning, she made for the door, leaving Rolf staring. 'Something wrong, Carla?' His voice was his own, but still she ran, finding Blaze's office and pressing her trembling lips.

The past was haunting her as it had before. Her marriage to Blaze hadn't exorcised it, after all. Was it because he still blamed her for what had happened to Crispin? Was it so much in Blaze's mind that she had picked up his thoughts by telepathy, because that was the room, the ballroom, where that terrible night had started?

There seemed to be a quarrel. Hard words drifted in. Blaze was swearing at Rolf—*at Rolf*? But he had been helping Blaze, he'd said, making sure the equipment worked. The door was thrust open and Blaze stood there, bayoneting her with his stare.

'You two-timing little bitch! All these weeks you've been in league with Rolf Horner!' She turned her trembling limbs away from him, but he seized her wrist and swung her round. 'No wonder you were standing in the garden alone, looking on and waiting—waiting for that moment when those things in there were demonstrated—and *nothing happened*!'

Bewildered, Carla shook her head, guessing that words would do nothing to help her. He would not listen to denials of collaboration. 'Rolf said he was testing them to make sure they worked,' she offered at last.

'*Testing them*? He was sabotaging them, every

single item. He was making sure they didn't work!'

'You don't really think I was in league with him?'

'You were up to your neck. Do you think I haven't noticed how close you two have been getting lately? Be honest, if you can—you planned, through him, revenge on my so-called revenge on you. The man works for a rival concern. They're desperate to do me harm. What better way than for him to get you on his side——'

'I'd never be disloyal to you!' she declared.

'How touching,' he sneered, 'when you were talking to him in there only a few moments ago. Did you let him in, or did he use Janetta's key to my front door? She works for the same company as her brother, so she wants to destroy my company as much as he does. But,' he gripped her shoulders, his nails deliberately inflicting pain, 'we are not going to be destroyed. Do you understand?'

Carla could only stare at him, her cheeks drained, her eyes dry, afraid of his suspicion, afraid of his intentions.

Blaze tugged on her wrist, pulling her behind him, through the front entrance door and across to his car. 'Get in.'

Carla stood stiffly beside the passenger door. 'Where are you taking me?'

'To hell and back.' He advanced menacingly and she ducked into the car, slamming the door.

They drove through the opened gates and turned into the road. In a few minutes Blaze had driven through the half-empty high street. He made for the town where his Head Office was, the town where Carla had lived for so long with her family, then her brother.

'I'm going for the chief electronics engineer,' Blaze informed her curtly. 'He'll know how to repair the damage Rolf Horner's done. His car's out of action, so he can't make it on his own.'

'Does he live in the town?' Carla asked, trying to disguise the inexplicable fear she was feeling.

'In a village just beyond it.'

Her clenched hands were moist. The haunted feeling had not left her. Blaze was driving fast—as fast as his brother Crispin had done that night . . .

'Please slow down,' she pleaded, through stiffened lips, 'for pity's sake, slow down!' Her voice had risen from entreaty to near-hysteria.

'Sorry,' was the terse reply. 'Time is of the essence. Those guests are waiting for the big show—the flashing lights which, thanks to Rolf, won't flash; the instant words and figures on the display screens that won't display, the copiers that won't copy.'

'I'm—I'm sure you're breaking the speed limit, Blaze.'

He flicked a glance at the speedometer. 'Dead on,' he said.

She winced. Did he have to use that word? They started down the hill and a film of perspiration spread over Carla's brow. The street lights were on. It was almost dark.

Farther down, a lorry thundered, and Blaze sped after it. He was going faster. What if the lorry should stop, suddenly, without warning? Her teeth began to chatter and she closed her eyes. Opening them, she saw a car. Its boot was open and a man was searching in it.

'That car!' she screamed. 'You'll hit it! It's stopped, can't you see?'

'See what? Hit what car?' The voice came from far away, three long years away. He didn't stop. Instead, he accelerated. She screamed, held her head, then remembered what she had to do.

Straining against her safety belt, she stretched out her arms. Her hands grabbed the steering wheel. With all her might she tried to wrench it round to avoid the terrible crash. The grass verge—there it was—they must reach it . . . The steering wheel was locked into position. Nothing she could do would make it turn. It was the end. She screamed, piercingly and hysterically.

The back of a hand caught her a stinging blow across her mouth. She stopped and gasped for breath. There was blood on her tongue, inside her lips, then she slumped sideways in a deep faint.

'You nearly killed us both!'

Carla stirred, returning to consciousness and finding herself lying on the grass. If her mouth had not hurt so much, she would have smiled. History, she thought hazily, does have a habit of repeating itself, doesn't it? The conversation was all in her mind.

Hovering over her was a face. In the darkness she could not make out the features, but her feeling fingers tested their shape. It was a man, and he was familiar—very familiar. Her lover—*her husband*?

Opening her eyes, she stared at him. Her fingers touched her mouth. 'It hurts,' she managed to say.

'I had to do it—I'm sorry. You were reaching out, trying to take over the driving—from the passenger's seat, too!' A pause while a gentle hand ran over her cheek. 'I've heard of back-seat drivers, but never——' He lifted himself on to his elbow. The moon had crept from its hiding plaee and revealed the revelation his face reflected.

'You've realised?' she asked, near to joy. 'You know now?'

'Oh yes, I know—I know now the sequence of events! That witness thought you were distracting Crispin. In reality, you were grabbing the wheel, diverting the car to the grass verge where it was found, thus avoiding a terrible collision, plus saving the life of a completely innocent man.'

'Yes, yes,' she whispered. 'It's true what you say, every word.' It was like a terrible weight being winched away, a nightmare banished . . . The past had been exorcised at last! 'I really thought I saw that car, that man.'

Blaze's arms cradled her, his cheek against her head.

'I won't be haunted any more,' she rejoiced. 'Your belief in me has chased it away and I'm free again. It's wonderful, Blaze!' Her throat was choked with tears. 'You've no idea how awful it's been, married to you, loving you—yet knowing all the time you didn't believe I was innocent of your accusation.' She turned her head. 'Did you know I love you, Blaze?'

He laughed deep in his throat. All restraint had left him. 'I think that fact came over on our first night together, my love.'

'I'm glad. Do you know,' she went on, 'I think you're human, after all?'

'If this were the right time and the right place, witch, I'd show you just how human I am.' His hand cradled her breast, then he bent to kiss it. 'As if you didn't know already.'

Carla looked around, peering through the darkness. 'Where are we?' she asked.

'In a field. After you'd passed out, I drove like mad until I found a side-turning. It wasn't long before there was a farm gate. I parked there, opened it and carried you here.'

She felt with her hand. 'There's a rug.'

'From the car. The grass is damp.'

Her hand lifted shakily to smooth his hair. 'You think of everything.'

'I do my best.' His voice was smiling.

'All those guests of yours—should we get back?'

'No need to worry. I covered the possibility of a longer-than-expected absence. Must have been male intuition, to coin a phrase.'

'What will you do about repairing all that equipment?'

'All under control. I told my deputy to give the guests as much drink and food as they wanted, make some explanation, then take them in their respective cars to Head Office. There's a duplicate exhibition set up there.'

'You really do think of everything!' He smiled, then put his mouth against hers. When his hand feathered the sensitive skin beneath the fabric of her low-cut gown, she gripped his head, clasping handfuls of his dark hair as, with immense skill, he caressed her to the edge of surrender.

When he lifted his head, she lay back, breathing deeply, allowing the fires to die down. She wished she could see his eyes and judge his humour. At last, she ventured, 'What about Rolf, Blaze?'

'What about him?' So she had chosen the wrong

moment. He was becoming remote. She had to bring him back to her.

'I just wondered. Will you report him to his boss?'

'Hardly. It was probably his boss who instructed him to do what he did. I've heard rumours that his company is in financial trouble. We'll probably make an offer for their shares, eventually taking it over.'

'Then sack Rolf?'

'And lose that incredible company loyalty? It's too rare an asset to throw away. I'll probably promote him and make him work flat out for his money.' He paused, then asked casually, 'What does he mean to you?'

Carla suppressed a shiver. He was still drifting from her. 'No more than Crispin did.' She felt him stiffen. His muscles grew hard. 'What I mean is,' she hastened to add, 'Rolf is very like Crispin was, isn't he?'

'He is, but I saw that years ago. I thought you'd noticed right from the start.'

'Only this evening, except that a little while ago I had a feeling I'd seen him somewhere before. I hadn't. It was the likeness striking me, although I didn't recognise it.'

'Maybe that was why subconsciously you were drawn to him?' She did not answer. 'Do you love him?'

'As much as I loved Crispin.'

Blaze's head lifted. He was hard everywhere now, even his voice. 'What does that mean?'

'Which was not at all.'

'Yet you encouraged Crispin's suggestion of an engagement. And accepted his ring.'

For the last time, Carla dredged up the past. 'At first, I really thought it would work, although my parents were against it. I really liked Crispin, and I mistook this for love. As soon as I discovered we were wrong for each other, I ended the engagement. The engagement was a sham, though.'

'Go on,' he was long-suffering now, 'tell me why.'

'Crispin wasn't serious. Rolf told me Crispin hoped to—get me that way.'

'But he didn't.'

'Blaze,' she felt for his fondling hand and pressed it to her, 'you know that. As for the ring—well, I was all of seventeen. It was something to show off to my friends. It was expensive and colourful. They envied me and I loved it. Blaze, Rolf's been no more than a friend, too. He was someone to talk to while you were at work. I was lonely all those hours. I missed you so much.' She added earnestly, 'You know I wasn't in league with him?' He nodded, smiling. The hardness of him melted slowly and tenderness put his face to her throat. Yet now it was she who stiffened.

'Blaze, there's something I must know. Why did you marry me?'

There was a slight pause, then, 'Because I wanted you for my wife.'

He was so cool about it! His coolness made her go cold. 'Yes, but—why? You see, Janetta told me you swore you'd have your revenge on me, and you thought that marrying me was the best way. She—she also said that, since she didn't want children, you and I would have them, then—then you'd send me away, keeping the children, and marry her.'

'Janetta would say such things,' Blaze answered,

unconcerned. 'If you analysed her character by computer, it would take fright at the data fed into it.'

Carla declared angrily, 'She broke up my boat, Blaze. She told me.'

'Good grief, she must have hated you!' Blaze stroked Carla's hair. 'Maybe you understand what I mean now about her character?' Carla smiled. 'Better to have broken up your boat, my love,' he said softly, 'than to have broken you. The motive was jealousy. You realise that?'

Carla nodded and lay still for a few minutes, then ventured, 'Rolf told me you had a plan to get me.'

He took his time in answering, kissing her throat until her body tingled. 'Yes, I had a plan,' he admitted. 'That terrible night, when I saw you and Crispin lying side by side on the grass, not knowing whether you would live or die, I looked at you for a long, long time.'

'I saw you,' she confided. 'All that time, I've remembered your face. I just couldn't forget you. You kept appearing in my dreams, but you always faded before I could reach you.'

He smiled and continued, 'I have to say it—I was furious with you for what you'd done—or what I thought you'd done—to my brother. Yes, I did vow vengeance. Then something inside me overruled my determination to tear you apart. As time passed, I couldn't forget *you*. I went to see you in hospital.'

Carla smiled. 'You thought I was asleep, but I saw you.'

He flicked her chin. 'I had your address from the police. One day, when I'd managed to "forgive" you, I planned to contact you.' He tugged at her hair.

'It so happened that you contacted me first, in a very unconventional way.'

She laughed. 'How did you know where I was moored?'

'Your boat was on my land. And I've known all the time. From the moment I saw a girl with rich red-gold hair staring at my house, I've known. One evening, I stood on the suspension bridge and watched where you were making for. Your boat was tied up not very far from the Boat Club. You took it upriver and tied it there—on my land. After that, I watched you often. You always returned to the same place.'

'So I must have passed you on the bridge?'

'A number of times. I could have stretched out my hand and caught you.'

'You didn't catch me, did you?' she provoked.

'No, but I've caught you now.' He moved across her and his arms slid under her body. He rolled her on to her side and they lay, her face against his chest, his lips on her hair.

'Blaze,' she murmured, hearing the hammering of his heart beneath her ear, 'please tell me the truth about Janetta. I've watched you two together, and I'm—I'm sure you're more than friends.'

He laughed, and the rumble was like thunder in Carla's head. 'You want a full confession of my conquests? Oh no, my girl! But this I will say. In the past, she attracted me—physically.' He felt her tension as his hand traced the outline of her body. 'I have the usual male feelings, my love.'

'Sorry,' Carla whispered. 'I'm not usually so naïve.'

He went on, 'It didn't take long before her attractions started to pall. You see, she had no intellect and no wit—no fun—to back them up, to add the spice of mental agility to——' he found her eyes in the moonlight and assessed their receptivity, 'to physical agility. Are you receiving me, Mrs Douglas?'

'Yes, Mr Douglas.'

'I'm paying you the biggest compliment I could pay to any woman, Mrs Douglas. You see, for me, you have the lot—everything I could ever want in a wife. You have my love, my enduring love, Carla mine, something I've never before given to a woman.'

He shifted and she felt his growing desire. Her arms curled round his neck. 'Why, thank you, Mr Douglas, darling.'

Their lips met and she delighted in the possessive hardness of his mouth, his impatient hands, the desire in her that caught the surge of heat from his body.

'It's time,' he said thickly, 'I took you home.'

'"Home". That's a lovely word, Blaze. Just one more thing, darling. It's early days yet, but that—that family you want, and I want, too—I think, I just think we might have succeeded in——'

'My love, my own,' he whispered, his voice exultant, 'in that case, it's even more important that I get you safely home.' He said softly, holding her to him, 'Into my bed—and into my arms.'

ROMANCE

Variety is the spice of romance

Each month, Mills & Boon publish new romances. New stories about people falling in love. A world of variety in romance – from the best writers in the romantic world. Choose from these titles in May.

NORTHERN MAGIC Janet Dailey
MASQUERADE WITH MUSIC Mary Burchell
BURNING OBSESSION Carole Mortimer
MORNING ROSE Amii Lorin
CHARADE Rebecca Stratton
BLACKMAIL Penny Jordan
VALLEY OF GENTIANS Margaret Rome
THE PRICE OF PARADISE Jane Arbor
WIPE AWAY THE TEARS Patricia Lake
THE NEW OWNER Kay Thorpe
TOO HOT TO HANDLE Sarah Holland
THE MAGIC OF HIS KISS Jessica Steele

On sale where you buy paperbacks. If you require further information or have any difficulty obtaining them, write to: Mills & Boon Reader Service, PO Box 236, Thornton Road, Croydon, Surrey CR9 3RU, England.

Mills & Boon
the rose of romance

Mills & Boon Reader Film Service

See your pictures before your pay

Our confidence in the quality of our colour prints is
such that we send the developed film to you
without asking for payment in advance. We bill
you for only the prints that you receive, which
means that if your prints don't come out, you won't
just be sent an annoying credit note as with the
'cash with order' film services.

Free Kodacolor Film

We replace each film sent for processing with a
fresh Kodacolor film to fit the customer's camera
without further charge. Kodak's suggested prices in
the shops are:
110/24 exp. £1.79
126/24 exp. £1.88
135/24 exp. £1.88
135/36 exp. £2.39

Top Quality Colour Prints

We have arranged for your films to be developed by
the largest and longest established firm of mail
order film processors in Britain. We are confident
that you will be delighted with the quality they
produce. Our commitment, and their technical
expertise ensures that we stay ahead.

How long does it take?

Your film will be in our laboratory for a maximum
of 48 hours. We won't deny that problems can
occasionally arise or that the odd film requires

Mills & Boon Reader Film Service

special attention resulting in a short delay. Obviously the postal time must be added and we cannot eliminate the possibility of an occasional delay here but your film should take no longer than 7 days door-to-door.

What you get
Superprints giving 30% more picture area than the old style standard enprint. Print sizes as follows:

Print Size	from 35mm	from 110	from 126
Superprints	$4'' \times 5\frac{3}{4}''$	$4'' \times 5\frac{1}{8}''$	$4'' \times 4''$

All sizes approximate.
All prints are borderless, have round corners and a sheen surface.

Prices
No developing charge, you only pay for each successful print:
Superprints   22p each.
This includes VAT at the current rate and applies to 100 ASA film only. Prices apply to UK only. There is no minimum charge.
We handle colour negative film for prints only and Superprints can only be made from 35mm, 126 and 110 film which is for C41 process.

If you have any queries 'phone 0734 597332 or write to: Customer Service, Mills & Boon Reader Film Service, P.O. Box 180, Reading RG1 3PF.